TOM CLANCY'S NET FORCE®

*Don't miss any of these exciting adventures
starring the teens of Net Force . . .*

VIRTUAL VANDALS

The Net Force Explorers go head-to-head with a group of teenage pranksters on-line—and find out firsthand that virtual bullets can kill you!

THE DEADLIEST GAME

The virtual Dominion of Sarxos is the most popular wargame on the Net. But someone is taking the game too seriously. . . .

ONE IS THE LONELIEST NUMBER

The Net Force Explorers have exiled Roddy—who sabotaged one program too many. But Roddy's created a new "playroom" to blow them away . . .

THE ULTIMATE ESCAPE

Net Force Explorer pilot Julio Cortez and his family are being held hostage. And if the proper authorities refuse to help, it'll be Net Force Explorers to the rescue!

THE GREAT RACE

A virtual space race against teams from other countries will be a blast for the Net Force Explorers. But someone will go to any extreme to sabotage the race—even murder. . . .

END GAME

An exclusive resort is suffering Net thefts, and Net Force Explorer Megan O'Malley is ready to take the thief down. But the criminal has a plan to put her out of commission—*permanently* . . .

CYBERSPY

A "wearable computer" permits a mysterious hacker access to a person's most private thoughts. It's up to Net Force Explorer David Gray to convince his friends of the danger—before secrets are revealed to unknown spies . . .

(continued . . .)

SHADOW OF HONOR

Was Net Force Explorer Andy Moore's deceased father a South African war hero or the perpetrator of a massacre? Andy's search for the truth puts every one of his fellow students at risk . . .

PRIVATE LIVES

The Net Force Explorers must delve into the secrets of their commander's life—to prove him innocent of murder . . .

SAFE HOUSE

To save a prominent scientist and his son, the Net Force Explorers embark on a terrifying virtual hunt for their enemies—before it's too late . . .

GAMEPREY

A gamer's convention turns deadly when virtual reality monsters escape their confines—and start tracking down the Net Force Explorers!

DUEL IDENTITY

A member of a fencing group lures the Net Force Explorers to his historical simulation site—where his dream of ruling a virtual nation is about to come true, but only at the cost of their lives . . .

DEATHWORLD

When suicides are blamed on a punk/rock/morbo web site, Net Force Explorer Charlie Davis goes onto the site undercover—and unaware of its real danger . . .

HIGH WIRE

The only ring Net Force Explorer Andy Moore finds in a virtual circus is a black market ring—in high-tech weapons software and hardware . . .

COLD CASE

Playing detective in a mystery simulation, Net Force Explorer Matt Hunter becomes the target of a flesh-and-blood killer . . .

TOM CLANCY'S
NET FORCE®

RUNAWAYS

CREATED BY

Tom Clancy and **Steve Pieczenik**

Written by

Diane Duane

BERKLEY JAM BOOKS, NEW YORK

TOM CLANCY'S NET FORCE: RUNAWAYS

A Berkley Jam Book / published by arrangement with
Netco Partners

PRINTING HISTORY
Berkley Jam edition / September 2001

Visit our website at
www.penguinputnam.com

ISBN: 0-425-18150-2

BERKLEY JAM BOOKS®
Berkley Jam Books are published by The Berkley Publishing Group,
a division of Penguin Putnam Inc.,
375 Hudson Street, New York, New York 10014.
BERKLEY JAM and its logo
are trademarks belonging to Penguin Putnam Inc.

PRINTED IN THE UNITED STATES OF AMERICA
10 9 8 7 6 5 4 3 2 1

We'd like to thank the following people, without whom this book would have not been possible: Martin H. Greenberg, Larry Segriff, Denise Little, and John Helfers at Tekno Books; Mitchell Rubenstein and Laurie Silvers at Hollywood.com; Tom Colgan of Penguin Putnam Inc.; Robert Youdelman, Esquire; and Tom Mallon, Esquire. As always, we would like to thank Robert Gottlieb, without whom this book would not have been conceived. We much appreciated the help.

1

Roy stood at the edge of the square, feeling cold and alone, and looked around him with the eyes of someone who was now a stranger everywhere he went. It hadn't always been this way. But he was getting used to it.

No one here spoke his language, Roy thought, but that probably was why he'd been given this job in the first place. *Less chance that I might understand what they've got me carrying*, he thought, only a little sourly. The idea that someone would actually send him off on a drop with a paper message was weird enough. He had studied the little flat-folded piece of paper in its plastic slip-carrier when he'd been alone on the way down here, leaning on a pole at the front end of the empty Métro car, but he hadn't been able to make anything of what he was carrying. It looked like a page ripped out of one of the old-fashioned hardcopy Michelin guides, incomprehensible enough on its own—printed in red and black, a bunch of little symbols followed by long passages in French, and a lot of numbers. It seemed mostly to have to do with restaurants, which only made matters worse for Roy, for he was hungry enough to eat a horse, which he'd abruptly discovered this morning that they actually *did* eat here. His stomach was going to have to wait, though. The gruff voice that always spoke to him from just out of visual pickup on the 'phone had been very definite—there was no telling exactly when the other courier was going to show up, and Roy was just going to have to wait where he was until she did.

Roy slipped the half-page in its plastic slip back into his pocket and glanced around him again. It was gray today, promising more rain. There had already been enough of it this morning, a steady depressing mizzle and mist that made the golden stone arcades around the square look grimy and tired. *Like I feel,* Roy thought, hunching his shoulders a little against the damp and the chill. September in Paris—it was supposed to be a pretty time. It didn't look that way at the moment. The month had been prematurely cold, and the last tatters of leaves were almost all off the trees in the square now; the bare thin branches rubbed and rattled against one another in the cold wet wind from the east.

At least there was shelter. The Parisians who had built this square and the perfectly matched six-story buildings that surrounded it were a patrician bunch, too aristocratic to want to be rained on when they went out. So the sidewalks in front of the buildings were under cover, the second floor having been built out over them, held up by wide sandstone columns. The ground floors of all the buildings in the square either had little shops in them, or were occupied by garages for the people living in the apartments above. Roy had "window-shopped" among them for a while when he first arrived earlier this afternoon, looking in at the soaps and perfumes in the perfumery, the expensive bags and cases in the suitcase shop, the extremely expensive suit and dress worn by the two dead-white minimalist mannequins in the couturier's window. But soon enough he got bored with that and drifted down instead to take his first look into the restaurant at the corner, where people had forsaken the few little outside tables, even though there were gas heaters above them, and were all inside, in the golden warmth of the place, drinking wine and laughing.

At the time Roy had smiled a little sardonically at them and walked on by. He could hardly remember the last time he laughed for sheer pleasure . . . let alone at something as simple as a joke. There'd been little enough to laugh about at home, what with his mother's endless complaining about how expensive everything was, and about how his father was late with the support payment again. There was never any peace at home, no matter what Roy did to try to make things better. His mother nagged him for not eating everything on his plate, and then nagged him for putting on weight. She nagged him for not doing well enough at school, because school was very important, and then in practically the next breath she would nag him for not quitting school and going out to get a job. And she didn't seem able to hear the contradictions in what she said. Pointing them out to her only got Roy slapped, and then seriously scolded for "talking back" and "being disrespectful," and then would come floods of tears and recriminations, his mother's guilt and anger and helplessness all mixed together and dumped on him. Roy often enough felt like having a good cry about it all himself, but the odds were much too strong that in their small apartment his mother would probably catch him at it, and he wasn't going to let his parents suspect that they had been successful in driving him to that kind of reaction.

He'd borne it as long as he could, but there came one night when it all just got to be too much. For once there wasn't any triggering incident. Roy just came in from school and found his mother in the dining room, sitting at the table with her head in her hands, and Roy knew it was going to be another awful night. *I can't take it anymore,* some part of his brain had suddenly said to him, with terrible clarity. *I just can't. If I try to, something awful's going to happen.* Very quietly, about two in the morning, Roy had moved softly around the apartment in the dark—he didn't dare turn on a light; he was sure his mother would have sensed it somehow—and gathered up all the things he felt he absolutely couldn't live without on a long trip away. Then he wrote a brief note telling his mother not to worry, and got out of there before it got any worse.

Now—standing here in the chill dimness under the arcades, watching the last few yellow leaves blow by across the pale golden-pink gravel in the center of the square, and whirl around the base of the fountain there—Roy had to admit to himself that he had been incredibly naive. Everything had gotten worse, much worse, immediately. Within hours of walking out the door, in fact. All the friends on whom Roy would have counted to give him a place to stay while he figured out what to do next now told him that they couldn't help him out. Reggie's folks wouldn't let someone stay with them whom they knew to be a runaway. They were afraid of legal complications. He went to Mike's and Dawn's and Lalla's and Will's, but there was always some other reason he couldn't stay with them—guests in the house, friends going away, relatives coming to visit, family trouble. It didn't matter, the result was always the same. There was no room for Roy. So finally he wound up having no choice but to go to a shelter.

Paradoxically, that was when matters started to take a turn for the better—at the point when he had been most ashamed and depressed at having to seek help from total strangers. Roy stood in the shadows of the arcade, stamping his feet in the chill, thinking of the first time he had stood at the door of the little Breathing Space center in Toronto. Strangers they might have been, but they had treated him with more understanding than people he'd known much better. Food and a place to stay were immediately his, and Roy was given a password and Net access to the Breathing Space virtual environment, a "place" called Haven. The only thing they offered Roy that he didn't want to take advantage of was the opportunity to get in touch with his mother. They didn't press him on the subject. He was glad, for he'd had more than enough of her for the short term—

A sharp clatter of sound out in the square brought Roy's head up. It was just someone's two-year-old, muffled up in a brightly colored one-piece inso-slick against the raw weather, throwing a plastic bottle into the fountain. Roy watched the child's mother leave the stroller she'd been pushing, reclaim the child, scolding it in what he assumed was French, and lead it away.

He sighed. It wasn't that the woman looked like his mother, particularly. But the thought of what that little kid would be going home to now—just the very idea of a home, a place you could depend on, where there was warmth and food and a welcome—filled Roy with a ridiculous nostalgia. He shook himself, as if the longing were something that could be shuddered away. He had other things to think about, other more important business.

Across the square he caught a glimpse of someone moving in the shadows of the arcade that sheltered the couturier's, and after the movement by the bundled-up, dark-dressed figure, a glint of eyes. A man. Someone watching him? *Not my contact,* Roy thought. First of all, the gender was wrong, and second, the men and women who sought him out on business these days were better than that—you hardly ever saw them before they saw you and slipped softly up beside you. This was probably someone looking for something else—Roy shuddered again, not on purpose this time, and not entirely because of the cold. There had been enough people who had seen him loitering around some quiet place in one city or another, during the course of work, and had assumed he was there for some other reason than dropping off or picking up small packages or obscure messages: something a whole lot more sordid. Roy had escaped almost all of them without incident, except for one. With that one, when he saw the flash of the knife, Roy had simply panicked and lashed out, somehow actually managing to knock the guy's knife out of his hand—sheer luck, nothing to do with skill—and had run for it. He had nearly missed the pickup he was supposed to make, and his "runner" had been scathing with him, threatening to let Roy go and find someone with more nerve. Roy had apologized profusely, and immediately acquired an illegal sonic.

He wasn't carrying it today, though. The French were paranoid about privately carried weapons these days, almost as bad as the Brits, and it was worth a long sentence to get caught with one. Roy had been specifically warned against it this time out. He wasn't too worried—as far as Roy was concerned, Paris was a safe and civilized place, except for the butcher shops. And now the dark figure across the way turned, wandered off around the corner and down one of the side streets that fed into the square.

Roy relaxed a little, looked up and down the arcade, saw no one; and out in the square itself people were walking through briskly on their business, or strolling by with their dogs. Roy made a little face as a brace of sable-and-white collies went by on the leash, pulling along their mistress, a hard-faced woman in a fox-fur coat. Dogs were all right, but the Parisians' attitude to where their pets relieved themselves was entirely too relaxed, and Roy had stepped in more dogstuff in the past day and a half than he had in Frankfurt, New York, and L.A. combined. He let out a breath at the thought of all the traveling he'd been doing lately, wondering if he would ever get over the jet lag. Half the time his body thought it was some other time than it really was wherever Roy was at the moment, and he always seemed to be hungry no matter how recently he'd eaten. It was a side effect of the jet lag, Roy supposed. At least it wasn't making him gain weight.

If I'd known it was going to be like this when I met Jill . . . But then Roy let out another breath and laughed at himself a little. Silly even to think, here and now, that he wouldn't have taken her up on her suggestion. He had met Jill maybe a couple of weeks after he got into the Breathing Space shelter in Toronto, while exploring the "Haven" environment. Whoever built that virtual "place" had been a real nature freak and had filled it with astonishing scenery, seaside and mountain vistas where you could just sit and relax and let all your troubles seem remote for a little while. The Haven was amazingly complex, and it would take even a committed explorer a long time to find all its ins and outs, but Roy had quickly discovered at least one, when he met Jill.

She had found him sitting under a tree on a hillside in some dusty golden virtual afternoon, reading from a text-windowed version of *Kim* that hung in the air beside him, while beyond it the mountains of western Alberta reared up, snowy-headed and looking slightly insubstantial in the low and slanting light. "Pretty," she had said, with no other word of introduction. "Boring."

Roy had looked up at her with some surprise. A lot of the kids using Haven were none too eager to talk to other people. After a few rebuffs he had taken to leaving them alone. But there Jill had stood, small and blond and sharp-faced and slight, wearing bodytights and ankle boots and a smock that rippled with changing colors as Roy watched it. She seemed unusually put-together for someone on the run from her folks, and she stood there looking Roy over with an intensity he found both unsettling and intriguing.

"Wanna get out of here?" Jill had said.

"I just got *in*," Roy had said, bemused.

"I don't mean *out* out. I mean, out of *this*." She gestured around her at the mountains, the impending sunset light. "This pretty cocoon they've put around us to keep us safe while we sort out our troubles."

"Why should that be so bad?"

Jill snorted. "Like the life they want us to go back to is so terrific. School. Living on a shoestring on whatever money your folks see fit to give you." Roy glanced away. In his case this was almost nothing, and the subject was so sore with him that he always avoided it. It was also the reason it had taken Roy as long to leave home as he had. It had taken a good while to pile up enough of what was laughingly referred to as his "allowance" to make even thinking about leaving a possibility. "And then working at some jerkwater job for the rest of your life, whether you did well at school or not."

Roy had laughed at her, poked a finger through the text window hanging in the air to mark his place, and had waved the window away to give Jill his full attention. She was pretty, in a sharp and aggressive kind of way, and her air of absolute assurance and spiky annoyance made you want to listen to her and see what came out next. "Like you have any better ideas," Roy had said.

"You'd be surprised," she said, looking him over again, with some attention to his clothes this time, and this time Roy blushed. He hadn't bothered to do as a lot of the other kids did, and make himself a "seeming" while visiting Haven—a fake somatype or a fancier representation of themselves, based on the original but taller, brawnier, prettier, more graceful, whatever they thought they ought to look like. The girl in front of him wore such a sense of assurance that Roy felt sure this was more or less what she really looked like. For himself, he hadn't cared until now if his clothes were out of date and showing signs of wear. Now, though—

"You need some money?" she said.

Something about her tone nettled him. "I don't want charity," Roy said.

"You're in a funny place to be making statements like that," she said. "I wasn't talking about charity. You like to work?"

"Depends on the work," Roy said. "If the money's good enough—"

"Do I look poor?" she said.

"How you look and what's real are two different things in a place like this," Roy said.

She smiled a rather crooked smile at him. "Maybe," she said. "Are you smart?"

Roy let out a snort of laughter. "Smarter than most."

"Come on, then," she said, "and we'll see."

She was so annoying, and yet so attractive, that Roy had gotten up and gone with her, without then even knowing her name. He had found that out soon enough, though. And shortly he had met, virtually of course, the people she "worked with," the people who were looking for smart kids who were brave enough to hit the road on their own and didn't mind picking up a buck here and there.

Roy glanced down the length of the arcade, and out into the square again, and seeing no signs of the woman he was waiting for, started to walk. Staying in one place around here for more than a few moments at a time was not a good idea. The apartments around the square were fairly high-priced, and the police presence here, his runner had told Roy, could be expected to be more alert and frequent than usual . . . hence the insistence that he leave the sonic weapon at home. "Home" at the moment, of course, was a coin-op locker in Gare du Nord, where the sonic lay well wrapped up inside his overnight bag. He would take the Métro back to the station when he'd made this drop, pick up the bag, and then slip into a public Net-access booth to find out where he was supposed to go next. The last time he had done Paris, he'd been sent down to Zürich on the new maglev TGV service and made a document pickup there. This run might be something similar. Or they might just tell him to go to Orly or CDG and catch a cheap flight back to Toronto, where they'd alert him when they needed him again. That had happened before, too.

Roy turned the corner of the arcade and started walking along the eastern side of the square, down toward where the restaurant was. He would have loved to pause under one of those heaters, but it would have attracted attention after more than a moment, and if there was anything one did not do in this job, that was it. His business was to be as colorless as possible, not to stick out in any significant way. That, Roy thought, was what had gotten him this job in the first place, when—after answering a truly mind-numbing and unspeakably nosey questionnaire with which Jill provided him—he "met" the people who were going to be paying him. The meeting had taken place in a quiet, plush virtual office which was not part of Haven, but which led out of it through a Net-portal into which Roy did not inquire too closely, since the Breathing Space people had said that such things were both not allowed and supposedly impossible. He had been carefully looked over by people he couldn't see more clearly than as shadowy seated forms, and the few words initially exchanged among his interviewers when he came in all centered around how nondescript he looked. It was, Roy now supposed, a compliment, if a backhanded one.

Roy never then nor since saw anything of his employers' faces. He never heard anything but voices which he was sure had been so completely electronically altered that there was no way he would ever recognize the originals. He had answered their questions with carefully concealed impatience—for they were a lot of the same ones he had already answered on the questionnaire, about his home life (nonexistent) and his relationships with his relatives (ditto) and his family income and so on—and finally one of the three voices which had been speaking to him said simply, "You'll do."

"All you'll have to do for us," said another of the voices, "is go places, and either drop things off and leave them, or pick things up and bring them back. You finish the job, you get paid. Pay varies, but we start at . . ." and he named a figure which actually made Roy blink and think he had misheard . . . but he hadn't. "Can we work together?"

"Yes," Roy had said instantly. And that had been the end of that meeting, but the beginning of what would be many brief exchanges with the third voice, the Gruff Voice, the voice on the 'phone with the source that always stood just out of video pickup.

The work had turned out to have its elements of drudgery about it, but it was still mostly worth it, though there were annoying moments . . . like this one. Roy passed by the restaurant now, just glancing in as he went by the windows and looked in at the golden stripped stone of the walls, and the couples eating and laughing together or single people sitting alone, reading as they ate or drank their wine. He walked slowly, so as to let the heat from the tall gas heaters at least drift briefly over him before he headed out from under the arcades to cross catty-corner to the other side of the square. Roy's stomach rumbled at the scent of steak and onions being sautéed inside.

Later, he thought, and then smiled the foolish smile of someone who catches himself talking to his own guts. But this was lonely work, in its way. None of the people you met for pickups or drop-offs was ever particularly glad to see you after the first moment of your appearance. Mostly, whether you were picking up or dropping off, they wanted you to go away as quickly as possible. After that, all that was left for you was the inevitable cheap hotel room— for you dared not expose yourself to attention by paying for a good one—and fast food wolfed hastily in train stations or bus shelters. Roy had become a connoisseur of this particular style of cheap-and-cheerful eating, and prided himself on knowing the location of the best and cheapest tapas place in Chamartín station in Madrid, the last coal-fired chippie in Dublin, the immense and inexpensive *bhaji* booth at the Wednesday food market in the Hauptbahnhof in Zürich, and the open-air *frites* kiosk in Brugge that had both the best "French" fries in Belgium, and (bizarrely) a Net-access booth attached to it around the back. But even at places like these, it was Roy's business not to stand out, not to become memorable. And all of this was interleaved with endless legs of travel—almost always public transport, paid for with cash whenever you could find a form of transport that still accepted cash, or otherwise, the cheapest possible flights on the "company" debit card they'd given him . . . cramped in with all the other denizens of cattle class, trying to read or sleep through the noise of crying babies, and once again, trying not be noticed.

But it still isn't all that bad a life, Roy thought as he came under the shelter of the arcades once again. He made good money, and had put aside a fair amount of it in the private account he'd established on one of his trips over here, in a little town in the Schwaebische Alps, south of Stuttgart. The thought of that slowly growing lump sum gave him a lot of satisfaction, after all his mother's insistence that she didn't want to give him money because "he'd just spend it." And now Roy was, to a certain degree, his own boss. He could take time off from this work whenever he liked, and stay at the shelter, or go somewhere else to have a holiday by himself . . . always making sure not to be noticed. The thought occurred to him, as it did occasionally, of how terrific it was going to be when he finally had enough money piled up to that he could just take it all home and show it to his mother and silence her once and for all, a lump that would plainly mean its owner didn't have to even *think* about work for about ten years. *But that won't be for a good while*, he thought. *Let her worry. The peace and quiet of not having to listen to her complaining all the time is wonderful. . . .*

Roy sighed, pausing to look in another of the windows, this one belonging to a chocolatier and full of exquisitely decorated and ornamented sugar in a hundred different guises. If there was a problem with the work, that was it: the eternal necessity to move lightly on these errands, to leave no "footprints" behind. And he also wondered fairly often what kinds of things were being dropped off or picked up by him that couldn't more easily be transmitted on the Net, in virtual meetings. *Information, probably . . . Though information can be encrypted . . .* Roy never went much further down that line of inquiry, though. It wasn't his business, and more to the point, he got the very strong feeling that it wouldn't be safe. He could lose this very nice, lucrative line of work . . . and something worse might happen. Better not to even think about it privately, let alone out loud to Jill or anyone else.

A sudden spate of frantic barking brought his head up again. Down at the end of the arcade, having just come into it from down the square, was the woman in the fur coat, the one with the dogs. The collies were pulling her along as energetically as they had been before. One of them suddenly broke loose from her, and she dropped her alligator purse.

Roy's eyes widened a little, since that was exactly the signal he had been told to look for. The purse came open as it hit the ground and sprayed stuff everywhere—

change, little cosmetics cases, a gold pen, a wallet. But Roy was briefly distracted by the dog, which came running at him with absolute delight and an idiot grin all over its face. He just managed to snag its wildly flapping leash as the dog went plunging past him, and braced himself so that it came up sharp, with a yelp.

He headed back toward the woman with her dog, slipping one hand into his pocket as he went, and as soon as he came up close to her Roy went down on one knee and started helping her pick up the things that had fallen out of her purse. *"Merci, m'sieur,"* she said as he pressed the dog's leash back into her hand. *"Je suis désolée, mon chien est trés mechant—"* She must have picked up on Roy's bewildered expression, for then she said, "I beg your pardon, sir, I am desolated, my dog, she is—I do not have the word, but she wants a boy dog very much."

Roy had to laugh at that. "It's okay," he said, "she didn't hurt me."

"I am glad," the lady said. "And very much I thank you—" She took the purse from him as they got up, glanced into it, and saw what he had been careful to put into it while shielding it with his body from any possible onlooker. "Yes, everything is there, I must get this clasp fixed again, twice I have had that done and it is no better—"

They were both standing up again now, and Roy brushed himself off a little, and was rather surprised when the lady suddenly put her arm through his. "You are very kind to help me," she said, "and my car, it is right here, can I drop you?"

He raised his eyebrows and couldn't help chuckling a little at the turn of phrase. "Uh," he said, not knowing quite how to react to one of his "drops" actually being interested in him after the job was done.

"Also now there will be a message to send back," she

said, "I can this way have a minute to give it to you? Yes?" She smiled at him.

Maybe there are some human beings out here after all. . . . "Uh, thanks," Roy said, "that's nice of you."

"This corner," she said, and while the dogs pulled and bounced at the ends of their leashes in front of them, together they walked to the end of the arcade and out of the square, turning down another of the little side streets that fed into it. About half a block down a long black car was waiting, a VW-Mercedes, and as they approached, a man in a chauffeur's dark suit got out of the driver's seat and opened the back door for them.

Without a second's hesitation the collies jumped into the backseat, and Roy smiled slightly at the sight of it as he got in after them. There was shed hair all over—this lady's chauffeur ought to be smacked for letting the car go out this way. As she slipped in behind Roy, the chauffeur closed the door behind her and got into the driver's seat again. *"Madame?"*

"The parking garage," she said. "He will be meeting us there, he will have the article ready. *Ah, mechants, á bas!*"

The dogs, however, seemed to pay no attention to anything their mistress said to them, and kept trying to jump all over everything, so Roy caught them by their leashes again and held them still, while the lady went into her purse again and came up with a pad and a pen. "They are wicked," the lady said as she started to write, "they are very spoiled, they have an obedience course that cost a thousands francs, but do they become obedient, *les nullos, mais non. . . .*"

She chatted inconsequentially to Roy for a few minutes more while writing, with occasional pauses to scrutinize what she had written. Roy resisted the temptation to spend too much time looking at where the car was going. Sometimes it was better not to notice such things. He spent that short time looking at the woman, and wondering how he had ever thought her face hard. It lit up delightfully when she laughed, which was often, especially when she talked about her dogs. Roy wondered briefly what it might be like to spend time around such a woman, maybe even to get her to smile at you the way she smiled at the collies. . . .

The car turned into a driveway, and its front dipped downward. A moment later it was dark, and the lady smiled at him, just once directly, ripped the top leaf off the pad she had been writing on, and put the pad and pen away. "*Alors,*" she said as the car came to a stop. "So now we are here."

The chauffeur got out and came around the car to open the door for the lady: She stepped out. Roy got out after her. The parking garage was like any other—harsh fluorescent lights, ribbed antisqueal concrete on the floor under his feet as Roy straightened up, after getting out of the car, and looked around him. What made it *unlike* Roy's usual experience with parking garages was that the chauffeur standing there had now produced a small but deadly-looking sonic, and was pointing it at him.

The man didn't speak, just gestured with the sonic at Roy, showing him the way he wanted Roy to move. Roy had seen this kind of thing before, and didn't panic. Some of his runner's clients were jumpy people, folks who were important either in the social or business communities, or more shadowy groupings about which Roy had his suspicions, and kept them to himself—criminal, intelligence, who knew what they were, some of them? His business was to deliver as promised, and keep his mouth shut.

There was a brief exchange between the lady and the chauffeur in French, none of which Roy followed, but none of it sounded particularly hostile. The collies were bounding out of the car again, and the lady caught them by their leashes and kept them from running off. "Over this way," she said. "Here is your message. Jacques? *Ah,*

*Jacques, voici le marmaille disponable. . . . le pouvre
faiblard."*

Roy turned and found himself looking at a beige VW-
Mercedes—the kind they used here a lot for taxis—with
its trunk open, and standing near it, the biggest man he
thought he had ever seen, easily seven feet tall, and not
skinny, either, but a veritable giant with cropped hair, a
dark face, a dark coat. Roy walked over to the car, not
much liking the way this was going. *If this guy's the
driver, Roy thought, he must get pretty cramped behind
the wheel. . . .*

Whether he was the driver or not, Roy never found out,
for the next thing he knew, the man had grabbed him by
the shoulders and whirled him around. The chauffeur
came from behind, grabbed Roy's wrists, and before he
even had a chance to struggle, pulled them around behind
him, crossed, and snugged a pair of readybinders tight
around them. The lady stepped forward and slipped the
note she had written into Roy's breast pocket, inside his
winter jacket. For just a moment while she was close, he
got a whiff of her perfume, a fragrance dark and sweet.
And the next moment, struggling—though it was too late
now—Roy was lifted up into the air without an effort by
that big man and folded ungently down into the Mercedes's trunk . . . and the lid of the trunk closed above him,
leaving him in complete darkness.

It was hard to know how long the ride lasted. Roy lay
there gulping again and again, ineffectively, his mouth dry
with fear as the engine started and the car started to move.
He tried to keep his wits about him, but it was hard. No
matter what anyone said, no matter how he tried to convince himself otherwise, Roy knew that no one who
stuffed you into the trunk of a car and drove off was very
likely to want you to tell anybody about it afterward.

For what must have been an hour or so, in ever-
escalating terror, Roy could do nothing but lie there, un-

able to move much, and afraid to try to thump or bang inside the trunk to attract attention, for fear that it should make whatever bad thing was about to happen, happen even faster. The blackness was full of the smell of tire irons and old gasoline spills and the cheap carpet they put inside car trunks, and lying there with his face against the harsh carpet, Roy tried to do a hundred things. He tried to think of a way out, to make a plan, even tried to pray and found that he couldn't even do that. The fear was just too great. And it was almost a relief when finally the car stopped, and he heard the driver's side door open, and close, and after a moment, the door of the trunk opened. *Now at last it's over....*

He looked up into the darkness, surprised. Somehow he had expected there would be daylight. What light there was was very faint, so that Roy saw only the faintest glint of it, bluish, off the blued-metal muzzle of what the driver held: and all relief and anger fled together in one last huge wash of fear. Suddenly everything was laid out plain before him, a long road that ended here and now, this second. Roy wished with all his heart that yesterday, or one of the days before, when there had still seemed to be endless tomorrows ahead, he had called his mother and just told her he was alive, and not to worry, so that if nothing else, she could have stopped wondering what had happened to him.

She'd never know now....

2

The sun was extremely hot on the back of Megan O'Malley's neck as she rode in a careful circle, eyes ahead of her, taking care about how she sat in the saddle as she came around toward the painted white top rail of the fence around the arena—a sight which, after three straight hours of this, was now causing her a mixture of apprehension and disgust. Her muscles ached, but that was the least of her problems. The biggest problem on her mind right now was underneath her, a problem called Alistair's Kingstown Walk Softly, known to his friends as Buddy, and to his detractors—of whom Megan was rapidly becoming one—as the Big Stick.

This was because he seemed to have a big stick, ramrod, or other such straight and inflexible implement stuck right down the middle of his spine. In a horse being trained for dressage—the art of riding a horse with seemingly effortless grace through complex steps and paces in the showring—this made for a problem, since one of the moves required of even beginners was to walk or canter gracefully and evenly in a circle. And at the moment Buddy didn't seem willing to bend his body into the slightest kind of curve. Nor was he terribly interested in walking in circles, either. Every time he got near one of the fence rails in the dressage arena, he tried to break out of the circle and follow it straight on.

Now they were approaching the rail again, moving softly through the sawdust in what for the moment was a tolerable enough curve. *Oh, please just do it right this time, just once,* Megan thought, more in despair than in any hope that it would actually happen. She concentrated on keeping her seat correct and looking straight ahead, rather than down between the brainless creature's ears at the spot where she would love to take a club and whack him, and at just the right moment shifted her weight in the saddle just fractionally to the right, just so, the signal for Buddy to turn. Megan knew that she was doing it right, she *knew* it, and sure enough he altered his angle toward the rail just enough, and began to make the curve, continuing the circle—and then at the point when he should have started to curve away, took another step straight, and another, and another—

Megan couldn't stand it. She reined him in and just sat there, looking around the arena, trying to find the patience to keep from saying all kinds of horrible things. Buddy stood there, chewing reflectively on his bit and looking completely unconcerned.

"What happened?" Wilma said.

"You saw! He just broke out of circle and started to go straight."

"You shifted—"

"I didn't! Not the wrong way, anyway." She let out a long exasperated breath, glancing around the sunny ring. "I swear," Megan said, "if I owned him, I'd sell this dumb cluck off to Amtrak and let them convert him for rails. He'd be more use as part of a freight train."

Leaning against the rails on the far side of the arena, Wilma snickered, then pushed off and walked over to her. Megan glanced around the arena, a duplicate of the one where they would be riding at Potomac Valley over the weekend—a rectangle sixty meters long and forty meters wide, surrounded by white three-rail fencing a meter and a half high. Under the downpouring sunshine, covered bleachers where all too many spectators would be sitting ran down both "long" sides of the rectangle. And in front of those spectators she and Wilma would both ride out, one at a time, on Buddy, to do their Level 3 routines. . . .

And die horribly, because the horse has suddenly become a waste of time, Megan thought. But she didn't say it out loud. There was still a chance of a miracle, or that something had gone wrong here that wasn't wrong in the real world.

Wilma came over to her, looked Buddy over. It was Megan's considered opinion that Wilma Christensen had more brains, as regarded matters equine, than any other rider she'd met since she got started sitting on top of horses. Wilma seemed to think good things about Megan, too. At least, they had hit it off instantly when they'd met a few years back, though they made something of an odd pair—Wilma short and thin compared to Megan's height and somewhat athletic build, Wilma blond and fair where Megan was tanned and brown. In any case, they had become inseparable at riding school, and later it had seemed obvious that they would start eventing together. *But neither of us thought we'd wind up with a horse who's overnight turned into an idiot*, Megan thought, *and a "model" who seems to be doing the same thing. . . .*

Megan wondered, though, if Wilma was having the same kind of thoughts as she patted Buddy and walked around him, looking him over. "Are you sure you're not giving him some other kind of signal besides the weight shift?"

"I am not giving the big stupid lump any signal except that I want him to go in a circle," Megan said, annoyed, "that being probably one of the first things that a dressage animal ever learns, and which he knew perfectly well how to do until about a month and a half ago, except that now he doesn't. He just glues himself to the rail and goes forward, like a train. A very dumb train." She let out a long breath. "Do horses get aphasia, I wonder?"

Wilma narrowed her eyes at Buddy as he leaned over and began to crib thoughtfully at the top rail of the fence. She poked his muzzle with one finger to try and stop him. He tossed his head and snapped at her. "Question should be more like, can one recover from being hit repeatedly in the head with a ball-peen hammer? Because that's what he's working up to."

"Yeah." Megan gave him a look. "You," she said to Buddy, "are nothing but a collection of potential cans of dog food flying together in close formation. Do you know that?"

The horse regarded her with an expression of complete unconcern and tried to start chewing on the rail again.

Wilma looked at this with mild concern. "Maybe it's his diet," she said.

"It's about as likely to be sunspots," Megan said, unconvinced. "He gets every vitamin and mineral supplement known to humankind as it is. And more than he needs to eat, if you ask me."

"You suppose that's the problem? Too much grain? It's late for grass bloat."

Megan shook her head. Her suspicions were far worse. "I doubt it. I think it's the modeling that's gone wrong somehow."

"I don't know if it's *that* wrong. The real one is doing the same thing."

"Cribbing?"

"Yeah, but not just that. The rail problem, too. All yesterday afternoon." Wilma's expression was eloquent of annoyance as severe as Megan's. "I was mortified."

Megan leaned on the rail. "You know, you might be right, though," she said. "If it's some obscure muscle or bone thing . . . the supplements wouldn't necessarily be enough to put him right . . ."

"Maybe it's why he keeps cribbing," Wilma said. "Minerals."

Megan sighed. "Without getting bloods drawn on him and having them sent for an analysis, and the figures fed into the model, there's no way to tell that for sure. If the model is doing what the real horse is, then the chances are that it's something weight- or motion-based. Which is unfortunate for us . . ."

". . . Because it makes it look like we're doing something wrong, instead of him."

"Please," Megan said. She was desperately tired of the way the model was behaving, but the Region One Young Riders Championship of the U.S. Dressage Federation was only four days away, and she dared not waste any possible practice time. The championship was a dream that had been some time coming, for Megan was not the kind to compete at something without a suspicion that she might actually make some kind of decent showing. She and Wilma had together been working with Buddy for the past year, and a respectable score in the championships had actually started to look possible. So together with various other kids from the local riding club, they had filed their statements of intent, paid their entrance fees, and had successfully ridden the qualifier test, the FEI Prix St. Georges Freestyle. Now they were in the final stages of preparation for the trials to be held at the dressage center at Potomac Valley. And all this would have been just wonderful, except that Buddy seemed suddenly and inexplicably to be losing several very basic skills which he and his riders were nonetheless going to be expected to exhibit in the ring, and as a result, both Megan and Wilma both now seemed doomed to be horribly embarrassed in front of thousands of people. Everybody who saw them would (as was only to be expected) assume that the horse's poor performance was something to do with the inadequacies of the rider, and she and Wilma were both going to die hundreds of deaths. Or at least so it seemed to Megan.

"Why didn't we go in for some kind of *virtual* sport," Wilma muttered. "One where you can just create yourself giant muscles and perform like a demigod, even if you don't actually have the equipment."

"Because any sport like that would be a dumb sport, one without challenges and suitable only for idiots," Megan said, "and we thought we were made of better stuff. Able to handle a sport with some rules to it, some rigor. We thought!" She laughed helplessly.

Buddy stamped and snorted softly. They both turned baleful looks on him. "Rules it's got," Wilma said, sounding grim. "Especially the ones that say it's too late to pull out and get our fees back."

"Who cares about the fees? What *I* care about is attempting to ride a twenty-meter circle on an animal who appears to have forgotten how to go in any direction whose path can't be laid out with a ruler!" Megan sighed as she leaned against the rail. "You want to give it a try?"

"I'll just kick him," Wilma said. "I did yesterday."

"You can kick the model if you like," Megan said. "It just complains about illegal instructions."

"I've had worse." Wilma swung up into the saddle. She looked good in the arena gear they were both wearing: black jodhpurs, black jacket, the regulation white cravat and black riding helmet. Megan sighed at Wilma's pulled-together appearance, for she was never sure that she herself looked like anything more than a female version of a popular lawn ornament, and the top hat that they would both be wearing in the ring on Saturday, for Megan, just made the feeling worse.

Wilma was settling herself in the saddle, and now began to walk Buddy in an "informal" warm-up circle, which to Megan's sudden rage the model now did perfectly. "I hate him," she said. "In a sport where the one thing you ask of the creature is that he do the same thing at least twice in a row, he just won't."

"Mmh hhhmmm," Wilma said, and continued to ride the circle. Megan looked at her thoughtfully. Her seat wasn't great—she was slumping a little—and she wasn't looking ahead of her. *Bad signals*, Megan thought, and nearly said out loud, but then she stopped herself. There were enough other things going on at the moment in Wilma's life which also involved rather confusing signals.

"Anything from Burt this morning?" Megan said. It was a question she had been avoiding asking for nearly two hours now, one which her annoyance at Buddy had helped her put aside.

"Huh?"

"Burt. You remember. Tall guy, blond hair, supposed to be practicing with us, canceled out at the last minute."

Wilma flushed red and reined Buddy in, finally looking straight out over his ears, but not at anything that had to do with the competition arena. "No," she said.

Megan looked at her sympathetically. "You should ditch him," she said. "He's making you nuts."

"It's not like he doesn't have reason," Wilma said. "You should have heard his folks—"

"I understand that his parents don't seem to be the world's best," Megan said, "and I feel for him, but, jeez, Wil, he passes twice as much of the grief on to you as he gets himself! I hear him when we're out together . . . and it's more than I'd put up with."

"You don't feel about him the way I do," Wilma said, in a rather small voice.

Megan restrained herself mightily from saying *Thank God!* Instead she said, "Look. He could at least message us, or send a virtmail, if he's not going to make practice. This isn't a big matter of the heart, it's just, you know, life and death stuff."

Wilma had to laugh at that, though the sound was pained. "I suppose. I'll mention it to him."

"Sounds good. So go ahead, let's give it a try. Track right, turn down the centerline at A, leg yield left D to S, then come back and halt at X."

"Right. Put the aids up?"

"Oh, sure. Workspace—"

"Listening."

"Guides on, please."

"Guides on." Immediately, faintly burning red letters of the alphabet, A through S with some omissions, and the letter X, now manifested themselves around the edges of the competition arena, and in a straight line down the middle of the sawdust, hanging in the air about a meter and a half high. These were the markers that told you where to start a move or series of moves and where to stop them. In competition it was your business to know exactly how long it took you to get from one to another, and how many steps your horse needed to take between them; before every competition, you would see all the dressage people draped over the rails and searching intently for some twig or leaf or post-mark in that particular arena that corresponded to the lettered spots in the arena in their heads.

"Okay," Megan said. "Go."

Buddy moved smoothly forward. *That's the way it should look*, Megan thought, *no obvious moves, no obvious weight shift, everything subtle, the horse going smooth*. At least the model was behaving at the moment.

This had been her own project, on and off, for the better part of the last six months: building a virtual "model" of Buddy, doing the necessary physical and mass metrics to allow her Net workspace to construct a horse that looked, acted, and rode exactly like the real thing.

It was a useful adjunct to your (admittedly invaluable) practice with the horse you were actually going to ride, especially when there might be four or five other people qualified to team with the same horse, and all fighting to get enough practice time . . . of which there was never enough even if there was just one of you. With a model, though, a simulated horse, you could at least make sure your own moves were right. And you could ride the sim for hours at a time without stopping, if you overrode the "reality" constraints . . . one of the minor advantages to practicing virtually. You could ride it in the middle of the night if you liked, a process to which a normal horse would object violently.

The only problem was the actual design of the sim itself, which ran into big money. Megan had looked into the cost of professional character and movement profiling by some dedicated firm like eQuines Unlimited or The Horseman's Word, and had come away horrified. It was just too exorbitant to even think about, even if the family had been rich, which (as her father constantly reminded her) it was not. So Megan had started building the virtual Buddy herself, learning entirely too much about the art of simming live creatures in the process. He was a work literally in progress, and the only problem with it all was that Megan was an amateur, and wasn't ever entirely sure that she was getting it right.

She still wasn't sure. More, from the expression on Wilma's face, she got the feeling that Wil wasn't sure either. She reined in, stopped. "I'm not sure about the way he's moving. You want to turn him clear?"

"No problem." Wilma started to ride him back to the

point from which she would once again begin the pattern. "Workspace—"

"Listening."

"Model change. Transparent mode."

"Transparent mode enabled."

—and suddenly Wilma was riding a horse made of brown glass. At least it looked that way. The skin was hardly there, and the inferred organs inside were just vague shadows, but the details of the horse's musculature and bone structure could clearly be seen as he went. Megan got lost in watching this, and stood in the middle of the arena, turning and turning again as Buddy went around with Wilma on his back, watching the bones and muscles move, watching the nature of the motion itself, looking for anything uneven, anything that would reveal where the problem lay.

"Leg yield?" Megan said.

"Okay."

Wilma started the move, choosing the version which was usually done in the First 3 series of riders' tests, straight from the rail to the center line of the competition arena. Megan could just see her giving the signals: outside leg, inside rein, just a touch of each. Buddy had been walking straight forward. Now, keeping his body parallel to the rail, he began to walk at a thirty-degree angle from the fence, heading for the center of the arena. *He's doing this right, anyway*, Megan thought with some slight relief, for he had performed it correctly for her as well. *At least something's behaving consistently. . . .*

"Keep going?" Wilma said.

"Sure, why not? Take him through the next part, the traverse. Maybe you can sneak up on him with the circle and get him to forget to go straight."

Wilma didn't comment, just kept going. Buddy began to follow the rail in a way that was correct for once, haunches out, progressing forward though his body was turned sideways. *Smooth*, Megan thought. *She's really got the touch. If I can get her to show me that a few more times, maybe I can solve our problem—*

The air filled with a phone-ringing noise. Megan rolled her eyes up in annoyance at the blue "sky" and said, "Megan O'Malley—"

There was no image, only voice. "Megan, honey, hi, it's Mrs. Christensen."

"Hi, Mrs. C., Wilma's here. . . ."

"No, it wasn't Wilma I was looking for—"

That was moderately strange. Wilma reined in. "Mom?"

"Hi, honey. I was looking for Burt."

"Uh." Wilma's face went taut with annoyance. "He's not here."

"No? I thought he was supposed to be with you girls."

"Uh, no, Ma. We thought he was going to be, but he stood us up." Wilma's expression got even grimmer. She swung down off Buddy.

"Oh. All right." Wilma's mother didn't say anything further for a moment, and there was something strange about the way she didn't say it, so that Megan said, "Was someone looking for him?"

"Uh, yes, his mother," said Wilma's mom. "She called me."

"And she didn't know where he was, either?"

Another of those odd silences. "She said he was gone," said Wilma's mother.

Wilma blinked at that. " 'Gone?' Gone where?"

"She said he had taken some things and just left, and— Well, I don't know, she sounded kind of upset, and from what she said, Burt had been talking about leaving home, and, you know, kids say things like that, but they—"

"Oh, no," Wilma whispered. Megan looked at her and was astonished to see that she had suddenly gone absolutely pale. In the bright sunlight it looked bizarre. At first she thought Wilma was going to faint, but then she realized the paleness had nothing to do with any strictly physical condition. It was fear.

"I've got to go," Wilma said. "Mom? Hang up, I'll be right there—"

The call from "outside" clicked off. "Uh, okay, sure," Megan said, confused. "But listen, Wil, practice tomorrow—"

"I don't know if I can. I'll call you."

And Wilma deactivated her virtual-experience implant, and vanished.

Megan found herself standing there in the middle of the arena, alone in the sawdust except for the virtual Buddy, who stood there by her and then very gradually leaned over to start cribbing at the fence again.

"Workspace," Megan said.

"Listening."

"Shut down the Buddy model, please."

"Default save from this point, or save from other time/place point?"

"Default save."

"Done." The horse vanished, and a second later the competition arena was swept clear of his footprints, as if he'd never been there.

Megan stood there, her mind filling with awful things that she very much wanted to say, except that none of them would help the present situation, and besides, she could just hear her mother's voice saying reproachfully, "And after that, what will you have left to say some day when you hit your thumb with a hammer?"

"I can think of a few things," Megan muttered under her breath. "Never mind."

"Listening. Was that a command?"

"No. Sorry," Megan said, and then smiled, a wry look. She might think about all the rude words she liked, but she still caught herself apologizing to the computer, which, however smart it might be, wasn't *that* smart. "Revert to default configuration."

The arena, the sawdust, the sunny day, all vanished. Suddenly she was standing in her workspace as it normally appeared, as an ancient, worn, white-stone amphitheater, fifty rows high, perfect right down to the worn seat numbers still to be felt shallowly graven into the seats. But the landscape surrounding it was no olive-overgrown Greek hillside or dusty Roman plain. Methane snow, blurring into near-invisibility when the wind picked it up and blew it, lay powdered bluish-white all over the surrounding cratered landscape of the satellite Rhea, only going tarnished gold near the horizon where the light of a swollen, setting Saturn shed a cold, white-gold radiance over everything. Sharp white points of stars burned down out of the blackness, and the little pallid Sun away off to the left, just past the spot where the curve of the amphitheater ended, threw long sharp shadows behind the rims of the nearest craters.

Megan sighed, for once in no mood for the beauty, and walked past her desk, which stood in the middle of the "floor" of the amphitheater. It was covered and surrounded with little geometric solids, some of them hovering in the air and oscillating for attention, changing color or squeaking piteously for attention. Megan took a close look at a few of them, recognizing designs or color schemes that indicated mail from this friend or that. Right now she couldn't care less about answering any of them. She didn't see anything urgent . . . at least, nothing as urgent as the complete screwing up of the coming weekend.

"Save and break out," she said to the computer managing her Net workspace.

"Saved," said the computer. "Ending session."

—and then there came the familiar sensation like being about to sneeze, and having the sneeze fail, and then Megan was sitting in the family den, in the implant chair, from which, through the venetian blinds of the nearby window, she could see the afternoon shadows fading toward dusk. She had missed dinner, to no particular result as it turned out, and now her stomach was growling.

Megan sat there for a moment recovering herself and looking around at the bookshelves, the piles of books on the desk and laid face-down and open on the chairs—her dad was deep in research on something, and had plainly hit that point in the cycle where he was going to be untidy about it for a few days. She got up out of the implant chair after another moment or two, stretched, and found herself not as sore as she might have been. The chair's passive muscle-exercise routines were working better than usual for some reason. Then she headed out of the dimness of the den, down the hall and into the kitchen.

Dinner proper was over—assuming there'd been one. Everything was cleared away, and the dishwasher was running, in sonic cycle at the moment to judge by the faint chronic jingling coming from the silverware drawer next to it. However, the fact that there had just been a meal didn't seem to have changed one of the verities of life in the O'Malley household. One of her four brothers was in the kitchen, looking for something to eat. In this case it was Sean, all six feet of him. But about two feet of the six seemed presently to be missing, because they were shoved into the fridge. The rest of him was wearing a very trendy-looking black sliktite that made Megan suspect he was getting ready for a hot date.

"You done in there?" Sean said.

"Done," Megan said, "yes. Finished. Through." She plunked herself dispiritedly into one of the wooden chairs by the scrubbed-oak kitchen table and briefly dropped her head into her hands, rubbing her eyes. "Everything is going to pieces, and the world is coming to an end."

Sean, still halfway into the fridge, said only, "Good, then no one has to go out and get milk."

"We wouldn't *need* to get it three times a day," Megan said, "if all you guys didn't drink it as if it came out of the faucet."

"I'm a growing boy," Sean said.

"You're twenty-one going on twenty-two, your bones are through growing, so don't give me that!"

"Speaking of which," Sean said, withdrawing his tall blond self, closing the door and heading out of the kitchen and down toward the den, "what are you getting me for my birthday?"

Megan looked at the ceiling as if imploring it for help, but no help came. The door leading to the hallway, the den and the bedrooms now merely produced another brother, this time dark-haired Mike, in jeans and sneakers and a bodyform T-shirt presently radiating in traveling abstract calligraphic patterns of blue and green on navy blue. He also opened the fridge, put his upper body into it, and a moment later came out with a large stack of cold-cut packages. These Mike carried over to the counter, where he rooted around in a cupboard over the work surface, acquiring a bottle of mustard and a small shake-on container of the deadly chili powder that he had been putting on everything lately. Mike then got a loaf of rye bread out of the breadbox on the counter and began hastily assembling something that bore the same resemblance to a sandwich that the Leaning Tower of Pisa did to more normal buildings.

Megan watched this performance with the resigned expression of a farmer on some African savannah watching the locusts make their scheduled descent onto the landscape one more time. "You might leave some of that for someone else," Megan said, in a tone of voice meant to convey a very strong hint.

"Why? They'd just eat it," Mike said, finishing the building of the sandwich. He took down a plate from the cupboard, moved the sloppy and unstable construction onto it with some difficulty, and carried it out of the kitchen. Megan prayed earnestly for an earth tremor, but none came.

She sat there at the table for a few more moments. *I really should eat something*, Megan thought. But whether from the events in her virtual arena, or from watching Mike throw together his snack, her appetite was now completely gone.

She could hear someone coming down the hall again, but to her intense relief it wasn't another of her brothers. It was her dad—tall, balding a little on top, dressed in jeans and a soft work shirt with the sleeves rolled up, holding his pipe in one hand, a Holmesian antique "deerstalker" meerschaum of which he was inordinately proud. "Dad," Megan said, "I need your professional help."

"What's the problem?"

"I want to kill my brothers in some way that can never be traced back to me."

Her father the mystery writer raised his eyebrows as he opened one of the kitchen drawers and started going through it, apparently looking for a pipe cleaner. "I have a few interesting new methods on tap this week. But all of them require considerable preparation, and no witnesses. And your conscience will still pain you afterward."

"Hah," said Sean, heading back into the kitchen and shrugging into an overslick as he went. "She doesn't have one. Six days till my birthday, Meg."

The door slammed behind him. "You see my point?" Megan said to her dad.

Her father turned around, leaning on the drawer to push it closed, and began performing the nearest thing to single bypass surgery on his pipe. "Your mother and I have invested a lot in their educations," he said mildly. "I'd hate to assist in their murder before we see some kind of return on our investment. Unless, or course, you're in a position to guarantee that you're going to make a salary the size of all their salaries combined."

"Plus twenty percent," Mike said as he came in the kitchen door again, putting his own jacket on, "and my birthday's coming up, too. . . ." He hurried out the back door after Sean.

Megan looked after him in mild annoyance. "You see what I put up with," she said.

Her father sighed. "More clearly than you imagine. Honey, have you had a bad day? My keen eye for observation suggests there's a certain sense-of-humor loss in the air." He removed the pipe cleaner he was working with from the pipe stem, eyed the horrible color it had become, chucked it into the garbage can and went looking in the drawer for another.

"That's a bad habit," Megan said. "You should give it up."

"I smoke one pipe a week. I breathe more smog than that in a day. Don't try to change the subject, honey. What's the matter?"

She told him about her afternoon's practice, the malfunctioning model—assuming that the malfunction was its and not Megan's—and Wilma's sudden departure.

Her father looked down the pipe's mouth, took the stem off and began reaming it out again. "A little unusual. And her mother said—what? That Burt had left home?"

"It sounded that way."

"This the first you've heard of this?"

Megan raised her eyebrows. "Not as such." She sighed. "Dad, far be it from me to describe this as the perfect family—"

He gave her a slightly cockeyed look. "I wouldn't go quite that far myself. Especially since I pay the grocery bills."

"Yeah, well, that's not what I mean." She fiddled with the fringe on one of the knitted placemats on the table.

"You and Mom," Megan said, "are extremely good to us . . . compared to some parents."

Her father straightened, put the pipe aside. "Well," he said, "it's always dangerous to get judgmental about other people's family lives, their interrelationships. There are so many factors that make a big difference, but never get exhibited to the world at large. That makes it hard to figure out what's really going on."

"Not always," Megan said. "Dad . . . Burt takes a lot of . . . well, it's emotional abuse, really. There's no other word for it. His folks . . . I don't go over there much. We try to make ways for Burt to get away, because really, when he's home, both his mother and his father ride him constantly. There's just nothing he can do right. They find fault with every single thing he does, no matter how innocent. And when they do start finding fault, they really yell at him. Not just cutting remarks, sarcasm, or whatever. It's scary, sometimes. If I heard you or Mom ever make that kind of noise about something, I'd faint."

"You might be surprised," her father said, sounding dry. "I've heard your mother's end of some of the editorial conferences for *TimeOnline*. Pretty rough stuff."

"Maybe it is. But, Daddy, you've never treated any of *us* that way. I can't imagine what that kind of thing would be like, coming from your own parents. And Burt's been putting up with it for years."

Megan leaned back in the chair. "Lately he's been starting to mention not putting up with it anymore. Getting out. But Burt's never been clear about exactly where he planned to get out to. I don't think he had a lot of money saved, for one thing. If he's got enough money to move out, all of a sudden, I'd think maybe he'd robbed a bank or something. . . . I don't know where else Burt would be getting it."

Her father brooded for a few moments, turning the half-pipe over in his hands, then fitting the stem to it again.

"Are there friends who might have given him a place to stay?"

"Not that I know of. I mean, none who wouldn't tip his mother off right away once they got a feeling for what was going on. If he's staying with someone, it's nobody from school, I'd bet, or from the riding crowd. Someone none of us know." Megan began tying the bit of fringe into a knot. "But what's going to drive poor Wilma right around the bend is not knowing. She's seriously freaked already. If Burt doesn't at least get in touch with her to let her know he's okay, wherever he is, Wilma's going to get even more frayed at the edges."

And Megan groaned and put her head down in her hands. "I don't believe this is happening," she muttered. "Why couldn't he have waited until *after* the competition? What kind of person does this to their friends before they're about to do something so important? What kind of person does it at *all*?"

"Burt's kind, apparently," her father said, leaning against the counter and sucking experimentally on the pipe. "Yech."

Megan looked up, for this was an unusual reaction for her dad, but it was the pipe he was scowling at, and now he took it apart again and went rooting in the drawer for another pipe cleaner. "Well," he said after a moment, "this leaves you with an interesting choice."

"I don't see that it leaves us with any choices at all," Megan said, mournfully.

"Whether to let this ruin your competition, for one thing."

Megan straightened up and felt her mouth set in a grim expression. "I'm not sure the horse isn't going to do that for us," she said. "Even without Burt, things are looking pretty awful."

Her father raised his eyebrows as he worked on the

pipestem. "So even if he hadn't gone off wherever he's gone, you'd still have problems."

"More than enough," Megan said, and sighed again. "No, I see your point, Pops. . . . My life won't exactly come to an end. I may wind up looking incredibly incompetent and dumb in front of hundreds of people, but that's nothing, really . . ."

Her father's eyebrows went up higher, this time in response to her ironic tone. "I've done it in front of millions, in my time," Megan's father said. "That last review in the *New York Times*, for example."

"I thought you said that didn't matter, because the *Times* critic was an obsequious cretin."

Her father smiled very slightly as he put down the pipe stem and started working on the pipe end. "I meant that, first of all, he was wrong, and second, yes, he *is* an obsequious cretin. But lots of people think he's not, so I probably looked dumb to them." Her father shrugged. "They're not usually people who would have bought my book anyway, so I don't care what they think. It's the ones who *bought* it and didn't like it that I worry about. After all, I took their beer money and didn't entertain them. But third, and most important . . . how much does it really *matter?* In two hundred years who's going to care?"

Megan blinked . . . then sighed again. "Okay," she said. "This is that 'sense of proportion' thing you keep telling me about."

"When humor fails you," her father said, grimacing at the second pipecleaner and throwing it away, "there's no better substitute. Meanwhile, what have Burt's folks been doing about this situation?"

"I don't know," Megan said. "I should call Wilma and see if she knows anything. . . . I don't want to call them myself. I don't know them all that well."

"And from the sound of it, you don't want to."

Megan shook her head. Every time she had called Burt's house in the past, there had been the sound of shouting in the background, and once, when the phone was on visual, she had seen Burt's mother go by in the background of the view, looking grim and purposeful about where she was going, and carrying . . . She shook her head again. Surely nobody in this day and age actually hit their kid with a belt. She had to have seen that wrong. *Oh, jeez, I hope I saw that wrong. . . .* "It's not high on my list," Megan said to her father. "I'll call Wilma in an hour or so and see what she found out."

"And what about Saturday?" her father said. "Are you going to be able to replace Burt if no one can find him?"

Megan rubbed her eyes again. "It's not that simple," she said. "The team qualifies as a group, and everybody has to have been preregistered as part of a team with the horse they're working with. If we're incredibly lucky, we might be able to get one of the other riders who's certified with Burt's horse to fill in. But there's no guarantee that whoever it is will've been working on the same figures and patterns that Burt was preparing . . . the ones the judges are going to be looking for." She sighed, looked up again. "Dad," Megan said, "what do you do when you see a complete disaster coming, and no matter how you try to cope, there's just no way to avoid it?"

He was frowning at the meerschaum pipe, screwing it together again. "Prepare your responses in advance," her father said, sounding resigned, "and do your best to make them graceful. People do remember that afterward, no matter what the winners say."

Megan sighed as her father went out of the kitchen, and got up to throw herself together some kind of dinner, while thinking morosely about Burt, Buddy, her sim of Buddy, and the general unfairness of life. *I'd better get the nourishment into me now, because I'm not gonna have time in the next seventy-two hours. . . .*

3

Later, three days later to be precise, Megan was standing in the shade of the big stands at Potomac Valley, in the "prepping area," looking down at her photocopy of her team's points sheet. She was thinking black thoughts about graceful responses and senses of proportion, since her sense of humor had so completely deserted her that she suspected she'd have to take out an ad in the paper and post notices around the neighborhood to find it again. All around her, people dressed as Megan was in dressage jodhpurs and black jackets were making their way back and forth, leading dapper and well-groomed horses of every description to and from the parking lot full of cars fastened to horse trailers. Around the little brown prefab temporary buildings under the stands that hosted the administrative offices, the air was full of the smell of wood shavings and sweat, and also of occasional cries of delight from people who had gotten their aggregate scores and were not horribly disappointed. Megan was not one of these.

She leaned against the wall of one of the prefabs and scowled at the scoring paper as if a mean look could make the digits twist themselves into more acceptable shapes. Her team's overall score was passable . . . *just*. It was not because they had done all that badly as a group. Mick Posen had volunteered to fill in for Burt on the horse the two of them had been sharing, McDaid's White Knight, and had done extremely well for someone who had come to the qualifiers prepared for a completely different routine—but Whitey was one of those horses routinely referred to as "bomb-proof," a steady, untemperamental, and good-natured creature who would do just about anything you asked him, short of jumping over the Moon, as long as you gave him extravagant amounts of horse goodies afterwards. Their teammate Rick had ridden his mount, Wellington Donnerschlag Second Strike (also known as Old Ugly) as perfectly as could be expected. And after that, to her own astonishment, Megan had actually had a good ride on Buddy. He had come "off the rails," performing very passable circles and running through the rest of the routine in an acceptable, if not exactly inspired, manner. It was as if the big blockheaded monster had just been *pretending* to malfunction—as if all the trouble of the previous week had been a big act. But as soon as he got out in front of the crowd, he began behaving like a well-oiled machine. *Maybe that was something I should have added to the simulation*, Megan thought suddenly, as she glanced down the scoring paper one more time. *The smell of the sawdust . . . the roar of the crowd.* There was no arguing the fact that some horses were performance freaks, egotistic critters who lived to be cheered at. *Something to think about for later . . .*

If there was even going to be a later. For, though their fourth teammate Joanne Fisher had done very well on Old

Ugly herself, then it had come Wilma's turn to ride. . . .
Megan resisted the urge to cover her face and moan.
Buddy had actually done pretty well, under the circumstances, but Wilma had sat him with all the grace and élan
of a sack of potatoes. She was clearly somewhere else
entirely while she rode. *In the loser's circle*, Megan
thought, and then grimaced in annoyance at her own cru-
elty. . . . *Worrying about Burt.*

But she had had reason. No one had heard from Burt
for three days now. His parents, according to Wilma, had
called the police, but the police had told them what they
usually told the parents of runaways. There were too few
officers to chase too many kids who had gone missing,
some of them for just a few days. Unless there were suspicious circumstances, they couldn't really help.. . . .and
there was nothing particularly suspicious about it. Burt
had simply taken off, leaving a note behind him that said
he just couldn't stand it anymore. Additionally, he would
be turning eighteen in a few months. If he didn't want to
go home again, all Burt had to do was lie low until then,
and after that claim emancipated-minor status under state
law, if he wanted to.

Not that I don't understand why he'd want to, either,
Megan thought. *But . . .* She sighed and let the thought go,
for she'd spent too much time belaboring it over the past
few days, and whatever her intentions had been, her practice schedule had suffered. She found herself wondering
now whether she could have done a whole lot better on
the suddenly-not-misbehaving Buddy if she had spent
more of those seventy-two hours in the saddle and less of
them consoling a crying friend.

But, dammit, Megan thought, getting angry at herself
again, *what're you supposed to do? What are friends for
anyway if they can't depend on you to be there when they
need someone to cry on?* She folded her arms and hugged
herself a little in annoyance. *It's all so damn unfair. . . .*

"Megan!"

Oh, what now, Megan thought, and then once more angrily stomped on the thought as unworthy, and turned. Wilma was running toward her, and the difference between the droopy, sad, furious Wilma of a hour or so ago and this present one was astonishing. She was glowing, she was grinning all over her face, she was transformed. It was amazing, and a little annoying as well.

"What?" Megan said as Wilma ran up to her. "They change our marks or something?"

She immediately regretted having said it, but Wilma was bouncing up and down as if she hadn't even heard it. "He called! *He called!*"

"Who, *Burt?*" She blinked. "Just *now??*"

"On my mobile. He said he didn't want to worry me while I was getting ready for the competition," Wilma said. She was still actually grinning as she said it.

Megan could do little but stare at Wilma in astonishment, for the complete backwardness of Burt's reasoning simply filled her with awe. *It's true,* she thought. *It's true what they say. Males and females really are members of different species. I always thought my brothers were alien beings . . . now I know it's true. And as for Burt . . . !* She took a long deep breath, reached out and grabbed Wilma's arms to stop her jumping up and down, and said, "So *where is he?*"

"He wouldn't say, but that's normal. He's at one of the Breathing Space facilities."

Megan had heard of these once or twice. They were a kind of combined online-offline refuge for kids who were having troubles at home and needed a "neutral" space to renegotiate the business of putting their family lives back together. Right now, though, all Megan felt able to do was sag against the side of the little prefab building and let out a long breath of complete relief that Burt wasn't dead in a ditch somewhere. *Later,* she thought, *after I have a few words with him, he may wish he was.* . . . But that could wait.

She looked at Wilma, whose face also reflected that great relief. "So," she said, and shook Wilma a little. "You feeling a little better now?"

"A *little* better!!"

"Yeah." Megan sighed.

Wilma did, too. "I wish I'd known about this two hours ago," she said.

"Yeah, I wish you had, too. . . ."

"Megan." Wilma's face fell. "Oh, Megan, I'm so sorry, I messed everything up so completely—"

Megan restrained herself from saying what she thought. "Look," she said. "It's not the end of the world. They'll let us ride it again in three months. By then the season will've quieted down, there won't be any rush about it, and not so much competition. . . ."

"And this time," Wilma said, "we can ride it with Burt." The satisfaction, the relief on her face, were complete. Megan kept her face as completely still as she could, for her first thought was, *Will he be in any position to ride it?* His parents would be furious with Burt for doing what he had done . . . what he had been threatening to do, if quietly, for so long. If he did come home, would he find himself permanently grounded until he graduated? That would leave the team as badly off as it was already. Would they possibly even just throw him out to find his own place . . . ? Dressage practice would be the least of his problems, if that happened—

She sighed and shook Wilma by the upper arms again, in a companionable way. "Wil," Megan said, "get a grip. Let's go have a talk with him and see how he is first. Will they let us do that?"

"Yeah," Wilma said, "I think so. He left me a 'non-designated' Net address to check in with—it's both a message drop and a meeting space."

"Great," Megan said. "So let's see to the animals, and then get ourselves out of here."

Wilma nodded. "We'll be back," she said, turning, "and this time we'll get it right."

As long as you're still going out with Burt, Megan thought, *I wish I could be sure.* . . . But she sighed, and said nothing, and went after her friend.

Much later Megan got home to find her mother sitting in the kitchen. The kitchen table was covered with printouts, a few books, a couple of research pads presently showing pages from what looked like legal documents, and what was almost certainly about her tenth cup of tea. Megan's mother and tea, the blacker the better, were in a love-hate relationship that turned into "hate" about nine P.M., the time at which it was no longer safe for her mother to drink tea if she intended to sleep. *Not that she stops drinking it then*, Megan thought, with some amusement, as she glanced at the slender little blond woman hunched over the paperwork, dropped her dressage jacket over the back of one of the chairs, and dumped her helmet on the seat.

"Daddy's stuff all over the office again?" Megan said.

"Mmmh," her mother said, making a note on one of the pads, and then looked up. "Why can't people be *tidy* when they're working?"

Megan gave the surface of the table a meaningful look, which her mother caught and raised her eyebrows. "There's method to my madness," she said. "Whereas in your father's case, I still have my doubts. How did you do?"

Megan pulled the scoring paper out of her jacket's inside pocket and handed it to her mother, then went to get herself some iced tea from the fridge. Her mom unfolded the scoring sheet and gazed at it thoughtfully for a moment.

"Daughter mine," she said, "this looks like Linear B to

me. But I gather from the look on your face that things didn't go the way you planned."

"We came in twelfth of thirty teams," Megan said. "And you're right, this wasn't what I had in mind. On the other hand, it turns out that Burt is okay."

"Is he!" her mother said. "Where is he?"

"Physically? I don't know," Megan said. "One of the Breathing Space facilities, though."

Her mother sat back in the kitchen chair and twisted herself around a little in an unsuccessful attempt to get comfortable. "That could mean any one of twelve different cities," she said. "You going to look in on him?"

"As soon as I have a shower."

"I smell a horse," said a voice from down the hall. "And guess what? *It's my sister!*"

"Let me kill him a little, Mom," Megan said, glaring down the hall. "Just a little. I promise I won't do anything permanent."

"I've heard that one before," her mother said. "No, honey, it would start out with the best of intentions, but it wouldn't stop there. Let him live for the moment. We can only hope to collect on his life insurance at a later date."

Megan smiled a small thin smile, for her mother's tone of voice suggested that the boys might have been getting on her nerves today as well. "Is the Net link in the den free?"

"I don't recall it having been *free* for the better part of this century," her mother said, smiling slightly and turning her attention back to her paperwork, "but if you find any of your brothers in there, go ahead and throw them out. I've heard nothing but sarcasm from them all day . . . and after your father and I fed them for so long, too. You'd think gratitude was dead."

"After eating Dad's cooking," said another voice from down the hall, *"we're* the ones who should be dead. He did that thing with the chilies again, last night. *Bleaugh!*"

Megan and her mother exchanged a sardonic look. "Is this the new article for *TimeOnline?*" she said.

"No," her mother said, with some bemusement, "that one's finished. Would you believe *Bon Appétit* asked me to do a feature on copyright issues as they affect the great chefs of the world?"

Megan shook her head. "Weird."

"Not if you look at their price per word, it's not," her mother said, glancing at the fridge. "I may take up cooking in my old age."

Megan snorted and headed down the hallway to the bathroom. "Last warning, you guys," she said to the immediate neighborhood and anyone who might be listening. "I'm gonna be in here for a while. . . ."

The announcement was greeted with loud applause from down the hall. Megan grinned, locked herself into the bathroom, and spent the better part of half an hour showering herself clean of people sweat, horse sweat, and the emotional detritus of a mostly disagreeable day. When she came out again, dressed in jeans and a plain floppy white T-shirt, Megan felt positively human again, and this feeling was now not impaired by putting her head into the bookcase-lined den and seeing Sean sitting there hogging the big black body-contoured Net chair. He was staring into space and looking glazed, but this merely meant that he was immersed in some other reality, and for the moment Megan had no qualms about throwing him out of it. "Sean," she said, "I need the machine, pronto."

"Mmm-hmm," he said.

"Mom says cut it short," Megan said. "I have a real-people issue to deal with."

He blinked. "Like depriving your brother of his share of the household's recreation time isn't a real-people issue?" Sean said, turning his long self in the chair to look at her. "Give me another half hour to clean this up."

"Now," Megan said. "Clean it up on your own time, or when Dad lets someone else have a run at the office machine."

"Be well into the next decade, at this rate," Sean muttered, getting up out of the chair as slowly as possible and stretching himself. Megan heard joints creak as he did so, but she had no sympathy for him. If he was going to spend that long in the chair without tweaking the muscle-massage program to his requirements, it was his problem.

He then came lumbering across the room at her like some kind of slightly deranged Frankenstein's monster. "Sean, I don't need it right this minute," Megan said, but nonetheless Sean came at her with his arms out in front of him and an idiotically aggressive expression on his face that looked very silly on an architecture student. "Sean—!" Megan said.

"Arrrrrhh," Sean said, and Megan resigned herself to the inevitable as he came within reach. She stepped aside and took him by the right wrist, bending it back in a way that wouldn't hurt him unless he struggled. Sean yelped and tried to turn around in the way best designed to break the hold, but Megan glanced down and saw where his feet were—mostly very badly placed for any kind of balance. He tried to shift them, but too late. Megan simply knocked the side of her left riding boot against her brother's right shin. He fell past her, halfway out into the hallway, though at least he managed to roll as he did it.

"I keep telling you," Megan said with the slightest smile as she stepped over him and went into the den, sitting down in the implant chair, "leverage is everything. Keep working on it, bozo, you'll get it yet. . . ."

"I wasn't set!"

"As if the next mugger who comes along is going to wait for you to be set. You guys don't practice, that's your problem."

"Other guys have sisters who cut them some slack,"

Sean moaned, already well down the hallway. On his way to the fridge, Megan suspected.

"Other guys have sisters who don't throw them over the horizon often enough," Megan said under her breath, and smiled. She lined up her implant with the "eye" on the Net server box, closed her eyes, and did the particular muscular tic that brought the implant up.

She stood at the bottom of the white tiers of amphitheater seats, with a black sky full of hard white stars overhead, and the Sun, a brighter than usual star, now away off on the right, for Rhea had swung right around her primary, as she did once every six hours, and Saturn lay swollen and nearly full near the horizon—the planet's rings edge-on and nearly invisible, a glittering razor of light against the darkness. Megan smiled at the sight, but had no time to play her usual game with herself and try to work out what time it was by Saturn's phase and position in the sky.

She paused by her "desk," the white stone slab that hovered in the air at the bottom of her amphitheater, looking to see if any more urgent e-messages or virtmails had arrived since she was here last. Things looked more or less as she had left them, which was a relief, but then it was the weekend, and a lot of her friends were away, or busy with recreational stuff as important to them as her riding business had been for her today.

Though there was one virtmail, its iridescent sphere icon juggling itself up and down in the air, that hadn't been there earlier, and this one caught Megan's attention because the golden iridescence that tagged it was her signal to herself that it was from another Net Force Explorer. She walked over to that mail and poked it with one finger, and in the air off to one side, the message's address and routing information appeared. It was from Leif Anderson, who was the events liaison for a number of the East Coast-based Explorers who occasionally got together to do simming workshops or visit recreational Net venues as an informal group.

"Go," she said to the virtmail.

A moment later Leif was standing there in the virtual flesh, slight, red-haired and freckled, silhouetted against the background of his workspace, which this week looked like an ice cave. To her bemusement, behind him Megan thought she could see what appeared to be a Cadillac of the middle of the previous century, carved out of the ice. "Sorry for the group message," Leif said. "This is just a follow-up to find out if you saw the virt I sent out last week about the 'expedition' to the new dinosaur exhibition at the Smithsonian. Right now I mostly just need to know if you're going to be able to make it on the first date, the twelfth, since a lot of people seem to have schedule problems. We can reschedule to the nineteenth, but if we do we won't be able to have the paleontologics fellow from NatHist in New York along with us. So mail me, people, so I can figure out what to do about this—"

Megan sighed. *I completely forgot about this in the run-up to the Potomac Valley event. . . . I'll mail him when I get back.* She didn't normally treat her contacts with other Explorers so casually. Megan was acutely aware that the networking they were all doing now might stand her in good stead at some later date . . . like when she finally had enough credentials under her belt to apply to actually work at Net Force herself. The day couldn't come too soon, as far as she was concerned. Net Force was policing the cutting edge of life, helping maintain the collective sanity and safety of an existence that was becoming increasingly virtual year by year. And if things went well, she would be working with some of the kids she was seeing recreationally now; they were all acutely aware that as far as Net Force was concerned, they were all prime intake material. All she and her group would have to do would be convince Net Force's Explorer liaison, James

Winters, of that when the time came . . . and the best way
to succeed was for everybody to sharpen their Net skills
by working together in the virtual realm as much as they
could, in what little time was left from school and the rest
of real life.

But "unreal life" had taken a backseat these last few
weeks. "Got to do something about that," Megan muttered. Right now, though, there were more important matters to attend to. She poked the mail-sphere again. It
closed, and Leif vanished.

"Door," Megan said. Immediately a doorway appeared
in the middle of the space at the "bottom" of the amphitheater—an incongruous sight, since it looked like one of
the doors in her house, wood frame, a six-paneled wooden
door with a regulation knob. "Destination?" her workspace management program said to her in its usual dulcet
female voice.

"Wilma's space," Megan said.

Everything but the door's "frame" vanished. Through
the frame, Megan could catch a glimpse of something she
had always admired—Wilma's reconstruction of the interior of the Taj Mahal. It appeared to be dawn there, and
only the faintest pale pearly light suffused the marble interiors.

Megan stuck her head in through the "doorway."
"Wil?" she said.

"In here . . ."

Megan walked through, under the soaring expanse of
the great central dome, while outside the dawn began to
strengthen toward day. Wilma had told her that this vast
polished expanse of carved marble was "only for practice." The virtual interior she was presently working on
building was the one that even Shah Jehan had never managed to complete while living, the pure black twin to the
pure-white Taj. Jehan had intended to build this shadow
of the Taj's light directly across from the first building,

at the end of another series of reflecting pools. Wilma had told Megan that she was going to build it again in her virtual space, but not as just a copy of the white Taj. She had been researching the original plans, of which copies had turned up some years ago in the "Buried Library" outside Tehran, and was going to resurrect the planned building, along with the planned sculptures, as a surprise for Burt.

Now Megan strolled in under the slowly brightening dome and shook her head, looking up at veils and screens and columns of delicately pierced marble, delicate Moghul calligraphy and wall-carvings all painstakingly reproduced, and wondered whether Burt appreciated what Wilma was doing as a present for him. *If he doesn't*, she thought, *he needs his head felt. . . .*

But then maybe that's just the point. She wondered whether psychiatric screening was any part of what they did for you in Breathing Space. It wasn't anything she would have ever felt comfortable suggesting to Burt herself . . . but the thought had occurred to Megan, often enough, that someone who'd been through what he'd been through with his folks might possibly benefit from a little counseling . . .

She strolled across the marble floor to where Wilma kept the "work" part of her workspace. This was a replica of her home's dining room table, a massive thick-legged artifact of polished teak, its top all inlaid with beautiful light-wood curlicue designs that were the work (Wilma had told her) of an eccentric uncle who had lived in New Zealand. The ornate surface was covered, as usual, with school notes, notebooks, virtual pads like the one Megan's mother had been working on, and as always, a set of rolled-up duplicates of the Black Taj codices, three flaking-edged folios of ancient parchment written all over in Hindi or Urdu . . . Megan could never remember which was which. Wilma, in an electric-blue T-shirt and leg-sliks surprisingly tight for her usually more conservative tastes, glanced up at Megan as she came. "What kept you?"

"A long shower," Megan said, "and the inevitable brother. Dad keeps saying he's going to have them come and install another Net server, but somehow he keeps getting distracted."

Wilma sighed. "Tell me about it," she said. "My little sister practically lives in our Net chair. I don't know why she doesn't develop bedsores."

She straightened up from the paperwork and looked around her. "Hey, Rube!"

"Yeah, *what*, boss?" said an annoyed, gruff male voice out of the air. This was Wilma's workspace management program, which for reasons Megan couldn't quite follow appeared to be some sort of eternally irascible reincarnation of Wilma's uncle who'd made the table. For her own part, Megan preferred management programs to have a little less personality, but there was no accounting for tastes. "Hey, Megan."

"Hi, Uncle Doug," Megan said.

"Stop socializing and get busy!" Wilma said.

"It'd help if you told me what you wanted me to be busy with. I don't read minds," said "Uncle Doug," "and I don't think you're about to buy me enough processing power to fake it."

"The address I gave you," Wilma said. "Open a door to it."

A black patch about the size and shape of a door appeared. "Please note," said "Uncle Doug" in a changed tone of voice, "that this access is controlled. All access to the space is by express permission of Breathing Space Inc., and unauthorized accesses or attempts to enter or exit the space by other than officially sanctioned means will be prosecuted to the full extent of the law under statutes defining criminal trespass and violation of privacy according to appropriate state, federal, and international authorities. Persons with restraining orders filed against them are warned that entry into this space is regarded as physical approach in all states except Hawaii, Colorado, and North Dakota. Entry into this space indicates that you understand and accept these conditions."

"Right," Wilma said, "we accept, let's go!"

She went through the door. Megan went after her.

A moment later they found themselves standing in a large, bright reception area, as unprepossessing and impersonal as an airport: high white walls, soft white lighting from high up in a forty-foot-high virtual ceiling. In the middle of it all was a plain white desk with a severe-looking dark-haired young man sitting behind it. They made their way toward him, and he looked them over as the two of them came up to his desk.

"Wilma Christensen," he said, "and Megan O'Malley?"

"Yeah," and "That's right," they said.

"Here to see Burt Kamen. . . ." He glanced into the air to one side of the desk, probably at some data readout that the local space was set for them not to see. "Right. You ladies understand the rules? Don't ask him for information about where he is physically. That's his business. Other than that, there's no limit on visiting times—any time he chooses to have the system flag him as 'available,' you're welcome. The only exception to that is when he's meeting with family. The same entry combination he gave you will work for any further accesses, but if you attempt entry through any other Net address than this one, you'll be banned. Address control like this is the only way we can guarantee our clients' safety, and we take it very seriously."

They both nodded. "Okay," said the young man, "he's through there. Follow the blue tracer. It'll lead you to him."

A small spark of blue light appeared, and immediately thereafter, another door appeared in the air. The blue light drifted through it, and Megan and Wilma followed.

Megan, at least, had to pause for a moment to gaze around her in sheer appreciation as they came out the "other side." The landscape stretching away around them on all sides was absolutely breathtaking—some mountain range in the northern Rockies, she suspected. The hills running up to them, among which she and Wilma stood, lacked that manicured, managed look to be seen in the foothills of the Alps. *Someone did a really great job building this*, Megan thought, for she knew there was more to constructing a virtual domain than simply patching in a lot of 360-degree stereo stills. The wind blew, there was a faint fizz and hiss of rustling aspen leaves on the branches of the little patches of woodland surrounding them. The air smelled of snow and the pine trees that started farther up the slope of this particular line of hills. There was no one else to be seen for miles around . . . and Megan suspected this virtual "clear space" had been crafted as much for psychological reasons as for its sheer beauty and restfulness. It was a place made for people who had had entirely too much of the people closest to them, lately.

The little blue light was sailing ahead of them, through the aspen spinney and out the other side. The two of them headed after it, through the spinney, up a bare path through the grass to a gentle hillcrest, and down the far side. There was a single figure there, sitting under a tree, wearing worn jeans and a tank top; as they spotted him, and the blue light went sailing down toward him, the sun came out and flashed brilliantly on shining blond hair. He glanced up.

"Burt!"

Wilma ran down the slope to him as he got up, hurrying toward her as Wilma hurried. A few seconds later they rushed together, and Megan wasn't quite sure where to look, except not at them—for it can be painful to find that, despite all the good help you think you've been giving your friend, she has nonetheless just barely been holding it together. Now Wilma and Burt were clinging to each other, and Wilma was just barely stifling the sobs, but it was a close thing. Burt was hugging her hard, with his face scrunched down into her shoulder, and from the shapes into which his expression was twisting itself, Megan half thought he might cry, too. But he hung on to his composure, and after a few moments Wilma pulled herself together as well, and said, in a slightly strangled voice, "I was so worried about you!"

"You didn't have to be . . . you know I can take care of myself."

"Yeah," Wilma said, "but that's different from knowing that you don't have to be taking care of yourself, that you're all right!"

Burt winced a little, and then said, "If I'd known you were going to carry on like this, maybe I wouldn't have told you where I was. . . ."

"Nice to see you, too, Burt," Megan said, rather dryly.

"Uh," Burt said, and straightened up and looked at Megan with a rather more repentant expression. "Uh, sorry, Megan. Thanks for coming. It really is good to see you. . . ."

Megan restrained a sigh. Often enough in Wilma's relationship with Burt she seemed to find herself in the "advice-giving" position, having to issue reality checks to one or the other of them. It wasn't as if they didn't need them, occasionally, either, but sometimes Megan wondered how long her patience was going to last, since both Wilma and Burt seemed to need a fair amount of coaching in how to treat human beings they were supposed to be close to. *Not that I'm necessarily any great expert*, Megan thought. *But even a talented amateur can do some good. . . .*

"Obviously I'm not going to ask you where you are,"

Megan said. "But I, for one, wouldn't mind knowing where you've *been*."

Burt sat down under a nearby silver larch, and Wilma sat down next to him. He put an arm around her. Megan made herself comfortable leaning against another tree not far away. "I went up to New York for a couple of days," Burt said. "I had enough money to afford one of those stacktels they have near Grand Central."

Megan raised her eyebrows. She'd heard of these, an import from the Japanese market. They were "hotels" where you didn't so much rent a room for the night as a locked personal cubbyhole ten feet long, four feet high and four feet across, just big enough to lie down in for eight hours at a time. The stacked-up cubicles had Net access, but as far as Megan could tell, that was their only difference from a coffin. And the thought of sleeping stacked up in the company of who-knew-how-many other human beings, like sardines in individual cans, gave her the creeps. "How was it?" she said.

"Not too bad." Burt stretched his legs out in front of him. "I was scouting around for some work there . . . but I didn't want to linger. There are people there who can just tell if you've got nowhere to stay . . . and I wanted to get myself settled. So I found the address of a Breathing Space facility"—He smiled. He was not going to tell even them which one—"and used some of the funds I had left to get there. They've been nice. They kit you out with all the essentials right away."

"Like Net access," Megan said, looking around her again in open admiration.

"Yeah, it's pretty slick. . . . It's comfortable enough. The rooms are small, and pretty basic, but they're bigger than a stacktel . . . and safe. And there are a lot of other kids around to talk to."

"You could have fooled me," Wilma said, looking

around them at what seemed beautiful but completely desolate wilderness.

Burt chuckled. "It's not as empty as it looks. This place has selective 'invisibility' routines built in. You can't be seen by the others here unless you set your personal profile up that way. This whole area could be crawling with people, but you wouldn't know about it unless they felt like talking."

Megan nodded. "You've been thinking about this for a while, huh?"

"I knew eventually it was just going to be too much," Burt said. "It seemed better to have a plan for when that happened. . . ."

"But when are you coming back?" Wilma said.

"Back home?" Burt snorted. "Why would I go home?"

Wilma blinked. "Well, your friends . . . and you have to try to patch it up with your folks *sometime*. . . ."

"Do I?" Burt's voice acquired something of an edge. "Why?"

"Well, I mean, you can't just dump them. . . ."

"Why not? They've been talking about dumping *me* for almost as long as I can remember."

"Burt," Megan said, "that's kind of harsh. . . ."

"But it's true. Megan, you don't know them as well as Wilma does. . . ." Burt shook his head, looking out at the distant mountains. "My folks . . . they'd really rather be rid of me. You know they would, Megan! Wil's heard a whole lot more of it than you have."

Megan briefly flushed hot with guilt. This was almost certainly true, since she avoided every contact with Burt's parents that she could. "You get tired of hearing it after a while," Burt said. " 'You haven't been worth your keep since you got old enough to start avoiding your chores.' " His mimicry of his father's slightly Southern accent was bitter and precise. " 'Instead of you, I should've got a dog, and shot the dog.' " And he shifted tone, so that it was his mother's voice that spoke next: " 'All the other mothers have kids they can be proud of, but when your name comes up all I can do is tell them I made a mistake and I'll try to do better next time.' "

Megan looked away, uncomfortable. "You see?" Burt said. "You can't even imagine it. Me, I can't even imagine going home and *not* having people telling me what a waste of time I am. What kind of life is that for somebody? Sometimes I think, forget it, it's too late for you, they've got you programmed. No matter what you do now, it's never gonna work, you're always going to mess up, because that's just what they expect you to do. . . ."

He shook his head. "It's got to stop," Burt said. "If I'm ever going to make something of myself later, I have to get out of this, go find somewhere that I don't immediately look like I have FAILURE written all over my face in big letters. Somewhere where people won't tell me that I do . . . like they do at home, every minute of the day."

He fell silent for a few breaths.

Wilma looked at him, her expression turning more stricken by the moment. "You're *not* coming back, are you."

He shook his head.

"Burt—"

"Don't try to talk me into it," he said in a warning tone. "Even the people who run this place don't try to do that."

"What *do* they do?" Megan said.

"Oh, there's some counseling," Burt said, and twisted against the tree a little, like someone who finds he's leaning on a root, or an unpleasant memory. "That's part of the basic agreement. But they don't force you, they don't make you trade off contact with your parents for a place to stay. I checked that out before I came here." He sighed, looked at his boots. "There's some career counseling, too, for 'when your situation is stable again.' It's just code for 'when you finally give up and go home.' But I'm not gonna be one of the ones who do that. There's too much at stake."

"How long can you stay?" Wilma said, in a small voice.

Burt made a face. "That's one of the things the counseling staff won't usually discuss," he said. "They say that it's always handled on a case by case basis, depending on what each 'client' needs. But I've been talking to a lot of the kids here, and I haven't met anyone who's been here longer than about three months." Burt's face then acquired a smile, but it was a dry one. "By then," he said, "if they let me stay that long, I'll be eighteen . . . and after that it doesn't matter so much. I can go where I like, work where I like. And even now I've been hearing about some pretty good possibilities, things that'll be a lot more interesting than school . . . or trying to 'patch things up' at home."

Wilma's face was very still. "What about us?" she said after a moment.

"I'll come back when I can," Burt said. "Look, Wil, I know it's hard, but it's going to be hard on me, too. When I get a job, I won't be able to take time off any time soon. I'm going to have to work pretty steady for a while. And I'm not going to be staying around the old neighborhood, either. Too many bad memories . . . and too many chances I might run into my mom or dad." He shook his head. "I've had about enough of them for a while, and they've been saying they've had enough of me. We'll see if it's true. There sure haven't been any attempts by them to get in touch with me here." The bitterness in Burt's voice was once again sharp enough to cut.

"They haven't tried at *all?*" Megan said.

Burt leaned back against the tree again and shook his head wearily. "Look," he said, "I shouldn't complain. I've been thinking that I should have done this a long time ago. I've met a whole lot of other kids since I got here who've had problems even worse than mine. You wouldn't believe some of the crud they've been through.

And the one thing we all seem to have in common is that none of us can *believe* how long we put up with something that, if one adult did it to another, *they* wouldn't put up with for a second. They'd be on the link to the cops, or out the door, in a matter of hours. But some of us here have stuck it out for years, because we had no choice. We were kids, we were trapped, the system is slanted against us from the start, and there was nowhere else we could go, no one who wouldn't send us straight back where we came from and wash their hands of us. Or maybe we really thought our parents would change their ways somehow. We thought that *something* we did right would eventually make a difference. . . ." He shook his head. "No more of it," Burt said. "And I don't see why I should bother going back to school, either, at 'home' or elsewhere. One more year isn't going to make any difference at all."

Against such certainty, it was hard to know what to say. Wilma looked down at the grass, picked a small lawn daisy that she found there, and began pulling the petals off it, two or three at a time. "Look," Megan said, "until you at least finish high school, you aren't going to be able to get a job that's going to be worth much—"

"I've already found out here about some jobs that're worth a lot more than any job a high school diploma would get me," Burt said, turning those flashing blue eyes on her. "Come on, Megan! Think about it! As if a diploma means that much anymore! It'll get you a job washing dishes in someplace too small and rotten to have a machine to do it, that's about all. It gets you into college— if you have the money, and who has *that* much money?" Megan had to let out a breath at that. The only real tension she had noticed in her household over the past couple years had revolved around the fact that the savings plans established when she and her brothers had been born were not now yielding anything like enough money to completely cover their college costs. Her mother and father never actually fought about it . . . but the subject was often just *there,* hanging over other conversations, like a sword hung over the kitchen table by a hair.

"Forget it," Burt said. "If I want college, some day, I'll come back for it. Right now I'd sooner get out into the real world and find out what *life* is like, without people running me down all day. Make some decent money and stow it away. There are plenty of jobs out there. . . ." He trailed off.

"Come on, what *kind* of jobs?" Megan said. "Seriously, Burt, we're worried about you . . . we don't want you to wind up in some kind of trouble. And going job-seeking right now could cause just that. Sooner or later anyone who pays you anything worth earning is going to want your permanent address, and your Social Security number. . . ."

"Not if you're going to be doing the kind of work where they don't ask those questions," Burt said, sounding stubborn.

Megan kept her reaction out of her face. He obviously meant some kind of black-market or gray-market work . . . not usually the kind of job you would enjoy for long. She'd had no idea he was *that* desperate. "Look," Megan said, "Burt, think about this before you go off on your own. It's a big step. And you don't have to do it any time soon. They'll give you a while to sort things out. Maybe your folks will even see the light. . . ."

The look Burt turned on her was humorous, but at the same time made it plain that he thought Megan was out of her mind.

"I . . ." Wilma said. Then she held her head up, and looked Burt in the eye, and blinked a few times. "You deserve to have your own life for a while," she said. "I can wait for you to sort things out . . . if I know you'll come back." . . . *For me*, her eyes said.

The look Burt turned on her was heartbreaking. It was genuine uncertainty. "Wil, I don't know how this is going to turn out," Burt said. "All I know is . . . I won't be back to school this semester." He turned his head away, veering away from the heart of the matter. "And you're going to have to find someone else to ride the qualifiers with you. Later in the year, I guess . . ."

"We can find someone more 'permanent' to fill in," Megan said. "But, Burt . . . we're not going to be happy about it. It's you we're going to miss."

"Yeah," Burt said, and bowed his head. "I'm going to miss that, too. It was the happiest I got, usually. A good distance from home . . ."

None of them said anything for a few moments. Then Wilma looked up. "Can you come see something in my space?" she said, rather sadly. "It's not finished yet . . . but I'd like to see what you think."

"Yeah," Burt said. "Sure."

Wilma glanced over at Megan. "Go on," Megan said. "I'll catch you later."

Wilma and Burt stood up, took a few steps together, then vanished.

Megan sat there, looking around her at the superb landscape, and let out a long, pained breath. She had had the occasional boyfriend in her time, but she had never been as serious about any of them as Wilma was about Burt. Now she almost felt grateful for that. *It'd be terrible to feel about somebody the way Wil does, and then have them going through this kind of pain. . . .*

She stood up, dusting her pants off, though the gesture was hardly necessary on virtual grass. *And what kind of job is he talking about?* Megan thought. *Except for his riding, he doesn't really have any skills. . . .* Certainly there were jobs in the "gray economy" that would employ a kid Burt's age for a little while . . . but nothing that would give the worker any security. Not that it sounded as if Burt particularly cared. But there was something about this that was making Megan twitch. Normally, if Burt was going to be doing something aboveboard, he would have told them all about it, right away. Keeping secrets was not his forte. *I wonder . . .*

Then Megan shrugged. At least he was all right, and his skin was in one piece. If his ego seemed a little raw and tattered around the edges, well, he had an excuse. After the prolonged hell of being constantly told he was good for nothing, this must seem like heaven to him— professionals who were genuinely interested in him and willing to listen, a place to stay far from the troubles of home, access to his friends. If Burt felt like bragging a little about the possibilities that now seemed open to him, who was Megan to ride him too hard about it?

She made her way back through the beautiful landscape to the preset egress "door" which was standing there, pale against the sunlit hills, waiting for her. Once through it, Megan waved at the guy behind the desk, told the Breathing Space management system the address of her own Net space, and a moment later was standing again in her white amphitheater, watching Saturn slip under Rhea's horizon, only a sliver of rings still showing above. A moment later the Sun set as well, and with that small change of temperature, the moon's thin unstable atmosphere cooled enough for it to begin to "snow" frozen methane out of the lowest layer, which had until now been mist.

Megan turned her back on it and broke out of her virtual space, for the moment very much wanting some contact with parents she knew loved her, despite occasional friction, and brothers of whom she was very fond, no matter how much she felt they needed to be slightly killed.

A couple of hours later the brothers had taken themselves out of the house on dates or other business, and her father had emerged from his office to eat and relax a little. Megan took the opportunity to use the office Net machine, which had an implant chair she liked better than the one in the den, and made her way back to Wilma's space. *She should have had a little while to get herself back together by now*, she thought, as she carefully moved aside the piled-up books which, as usual, were blocking the direct view of the chair and her implant to the Net machine's implant link. Her father never seemed to realize that not everybody in the house was as tall as he was. *If she and Burt were saying goodbye for a while, she'll have needed it. . . .*

But after she had lined up her implant, snapped into her own space, and used the door in it to Wilma's, Megan found her friend rather more pulled-together than she had expected. Wilma's mood was somber, but knowing he was all right had plainly made a very big difference for her. "Now that I know he's okay," she said to Megan, "I guess I can get on with things. Not that I really like the way they seem to be going. . . ."

Megan could see her point. "You think he was serious?" she said, as they went out the front entrance of the Taj and looked down the length of the reflecting pools, still slightly vague in the advancing dawn, a light low mist lying over them in the moist, warming subtropical air. Down at that end of things was a great green space with nothing built on it, yet, and behind it only the low hills south of Delhi. Wilma had excised the modern city from this vista. "About not coming home, I mean."

Wilma stood there and sighed, and then shook her head. "I don't think so," she said. "He sounds so torn up—not at all the way he usually does. I mean, he's always been really good at coping with his folks . . . but he doesn't seem to be coping real well at the moment." She turned around to look up at the massive dome of the Taj, now flushing pink with sunrise. "I keep getting the feeling that he's just repeating stuff he's said to his folks, to freak them out . . . or that he's been telling himself, over and over, to help him stand what's going on. If he really had a more concrete plan, I think he'd tell me. I think he's just uncertain. . . ."

"You may be right," Megan said. "I hope so." She sighed. "What about this work thing? Were you able to find out anything more from him about what he intends to do?"

Wilma shook her head. "He didn't want to talk about it . . . said he was afraid of jinxing his chances somehow." She looked at Megan with slight bemusement. "I don't know why I think this, but sometimes it was as if Burt thought someone was listening to him. But he said that was impossible. . . ."

"Yeah," Megan said. "Well . . ." She sat down on a marble bench nearby. Wilma sat down, too. "I guess he'll tell us when he's ready. Our job is to make sure he knows we're here to talk to him and help him sort things out, if he thinks he needs help. But I think it's going to be a mistake to assume that he's going to ride the retrial with us, Wil. We're going to have to find a replacement for him."

"I know," Wilma said. "I just . . . don't want to start thinking about it right now."

Megan put an arm around Wilma and hugged her briefly. "Look, it's going to work out," she said. "You should get back out into real life and check in with your folks."

"Yeah," Wilma said. She sagged briefly, but then she sat straighter. "Megan . . . listen. Thanks. Really, thanks. I know I've been hopeless, the last few days . . . but just knowing that he's alive and somewhere safe . . ."

"It makes a big difference," Megan said. "Yes."

"I should go. . . ."

"Me, too." Megan patted Wilma on the shoulder, got up, and turned. "Door . . ."

" 'Door' what?"

"Door, *please*, Uncle Doug," Megan said, with a wry look. She glanced back at Wilma. "Why is your space manager so snotty?"

"Minimum wage," said "Uncle Doug," before Wilma could even open her mouth.

Wilma chuckled. "He was like that," she said. "I like to keep 'him' with me."

It occurred to Megan that Wilma might have done too good a job with this. But then, she had also done something similar with Burt, who wasn't that easy to hang around with all the time either. *Love is weird*, Megan thought, resigned. *Or is it love . . . or just habit, the tendency to want to prolong what you're used to . . . ?*

She waved and headed out her door.

4

On Sunday morning Megan woke up late with a strong feeling of having forgotten something, or missed something, something important. She lay there staring at the sun coming in her window slantwise and glinting off the Miro print on the wall by the window, setting the framed design afire in brilliant crimsons and blues, and tried to think what she might have forgotten. She couldn't come up with anything, except that she should really move the print before it started to fade.

From outside she could hear a confused mutter of voices coming from the kitchen. The usual discussions about the logistics of breakfast, Megan suspected. She got up, went on down to the bathroom and spent a short time making herself feel human, and then went to see about some breakfast for herself.

The kitchen was mercifully free of brothers. Mike's whereabouts were unknown, and Sean had decamped into the den to use the Net chair there. Megan went to the cupboard above and left of the sink and started rooting around for her favorite brand of muesli, and discovered, not at all to her surprise, that it was (as usual) gone before she had ever had a chance to get at it. She was unable to find any cereal at all except something called Choco-Hoots, and even that box had barely a bowlful left in it. Megan shook it disbelievingly, popped the package top open, sniffed it, shook it. There seemed to be nothing inside but sugar, something masquerading as chocolate, and some anonymous sort of crunch. "How do they *get* so big eating food like this?" she muttered.

"Has to be good genes," her mother said from the table, where she was sitting back in front of a spread-out NewSheet readout, over which the Sunday editorial "pages" were streaming. She pushed up the sleeves of her bathrobe, tapped at the readout to pause it, looked at it with an expression that suggested some editorial writer's work needed a critique, and began folding the readout up. "So, listen, honey, did you see Burt?"

"Uh, yeah." Meg turned away and opened one of the upper cupboards over the counter by the sink, in search of a mug for her tea.

"So how was he?"

"He seemed okay." She found the mug, and then a tea-bag full of the green tea with toasted rice that she favored.

"*That* tone of voice has 'disclaimer' written all over it," Megan's mother said as Megan went to get the kettle off the stove.

Megan made her tea, then went to sit down with her mother. "Yeah," she said.

"So what was the matter?"

"Oh . . . Well, just Burt, to start with," Megan said. "Mom, you ever have a personality conflict with some-one? The kind you couldn't explain rationally?"

Her mother rolled her eyes. "Lately it seems to be the story of my life."

"Well, I've got something like that with Burt. Just . . . a clash of styles, I guess."

Her mother shrugged. "It happens, honey. Never mind that. He's well? He's safe?"

"Yeah."

"That's the important thing. When's he coming home?"

"I think maybe he's not."

Her mother looked concerned. "Mom, it might be better if he didn't," Megan said, "if he's being truthful about the way they treat him . . . and I think he is."

"But what will he do? It's not like he's going to find a job that's going to be worth anything. . . ."

"I know," Megan said, and went off down the hall with her mug, thinking hard. She went into the bathroom, shut the door, started to fill the tub, and tried to think. An hour later, as she came out again, barefoot and once more in jeans and T-shirt, she was no further along toward working out what was troubling her.

She met her dad in the hallway, coming out of his office, also in his bathrobe and looking a little weary around the edges. "Were you up late?" Megan said, for he hadn't shaved.

"Yeah . . ."

"Done with the machine for a while?"

"Sure, honey, go ahead. . . ."

She slipped into the office and once again carefully removed the stack of books that her father had left in front of the implant, pausing as she set aside the stack to look at the title on the spine of the book on top. *The Gentleman's Art: 'Fiore de Liberi' and Other Swordsmasters' Instruction Manuals of Fifteenth-Century Italy*. And right underneath it, something called *War in 2000*. Megan wondered once again what her father was working on, and which war he was thinking about. . . . But her father tended to be secretive about these things until he was finished outlining a project. There was probably no point in asking him.

She flopped into the chair, lined up her implant, and blinked the world away. A moment later Megan was standing in the amphitheater again, and she made her way down to her desk. The same virtmails were hanging there in the air around it, but she had no interest in them for the moment, except to notice that there wasn't anything new from Wilma. *If she's smart*, Megan thought, *she's catching up on her sleep. She's had a pretty awful couple of days. . . .*

"Space manager," Megan said.

"Here, Megan."

She took a long thoughtful breath. "Link to the Breathing Space address accessed via Wilma's Net server yesterday."

"Done."

"Is the party referenced in the link available?"

"Checking."

There was a brief silence, and Megan looked at Saturn, rising now for the fourth time that day, and watched the rings slide up through the warming methane mist. "The party is flagged available," said her workspace manager.

"Open an access door," Megan said, and walked out into the middle of the space.

Her doorframe appeared, and the door in it winked out, showing her that Rocky Mountain view again. Megan stepped through and glanced around her. The "place" wasn't exactly in phase with the Rockies, apparently. It seemed to be late in some long afternoon, and the shadow of every tree lay out long across the little hills in front of her.

Megan looked around her, but didn't see Burt anywhere; so for the moment she just strolled down across the short golden grass of the small hill on which she had arrived, confident that the system would guide him to her. She was interested to see that the landscape was not as empty as it had been before. On nearby hillsides, and in the shade of the little forests and glades that dotted them, she could see people walking at a distance: tiny figures, some in pairs or groups, but the greatest number of them alone.

After a few minutes, when she still didn't see Burt, Megan sat down underneath the shade of a huge conifer of some kind and made herself comfortable on the pine needles. She knew that the system would have alerted him to her presence; if he wasn't hurrying about showing up, well, that was Burt for you. There was always the landscape to look at, and more to the point, the landscape architecture. She was running her fingers through the pine needles and wondering what modus the programmer had used to create them all, fractal or unary, when above her someone said, "You been waiting long?"

Burt was standing there, and there was someone else behind him that Megan didn't recognize. She got to her feet, dusting the pine needles off her, and was impressed by the way they stuck to her, as real ones would have. "Burt . . ." she said.

"One of the counselors snagged me just as I was on my way here," Burt said. "Sorry."

"It's no problem. Who's your friend?"

"This is Bodo. Met him a little while after I got in. He's been here on and off for a while."

"Hi, there," Megan said, and she held out a hand to Bodo. He shook it. He was an unusual-looking guy, maybe seventeen, shorter than Burt, swarthy, a little heavyset, and wearing one of the new contoured whole-body slicks that were so popular at the moment. Megan thought the shoulderpads and thighpads were a little silly, but she'd been keeping this opinion to herself, since so many of the kids at school thought the fashion too wonderful for words. Bodo, though, somehow managed to make the slick look good instead of just lumpy in new and interesting places. Maybe it was his hairstyle, which, though it looked strange with the ultra-new slick, suited him very well. It was a retropunk style with a long "tail" down the back and a close-cropped, crew-cuttish front, and the tail was dyed bright blue. "My blue streak," Bodo said, grinning, as he saw Megan noticing it.

"Bodo," Burt said, "is one of the semiresident geeks."

She smiled at that. "What do they need geeks for, here?"

"Geeks make the world go around," Bodo said. "As if you don't know. You look a bit geekish yourself, Megan."

"Me?" She grinned.

"I saw you studying the landscape. You do sims, don't you?"

"I've been doing one lately," Megan said, "but I'm probably not good enough to be counted a geek. Not for a while yet."

"There speaks the wise woman," Bodo said. "Someone who knows that geekdom is worth aspiring to."

"Wanna walk?" Burt said.

"Sure."

They strolled out from under the trees and downslope, to where a little creek meandered among the smaller hills. "Didn't think I'd see you back here again so soon," Burt said.

"Well . . ."

"Megan," Burt said. "You don't have to play nice-nice with me. I know you don't think that much of me."

Is it so obvious? Megan thought, in slight panic. *Oh, well . . .* "Burt," she said, "look, we may have our differences . . . but it's not like I don't worry about you anyway."

He shrugged, sighed. "Okay," he said. "I thought you would have brought Wil with you, though."

"She's a big girl. She can decide when she wants to visit by herself," Megan said. "And I had some concerns that I wanted to explore without worrying about how she was going to react."

"Uh-huh," Burt said. He shot a glance at Bodo. "I told you," he said.

"Told him what?"

"You were always quick to pick up on the unspoken stuff," Burt said. "You know. 'Work.' "

"That was exactly what I wanted to talk to you about."

They paused by a bend in the stream, looked into the water. Under the overhang of the bank, in a still brown shady spot in the water, Megan could see a gigantic brown trout that would have made her brother Mike run for his fishing rod. "Thought so," Burt said. "Look, Megan . . . you should tell Wilma not to worry."

"Why should I tell her that? You can tell her yourself."

"Because I may not be here to do it."

Megan blinked. "After all that, yesterday . . . you're not even going to stay here long enough to relax and get yourself sorted out a little?"

"I've had all the sorting out I need," Burt said. "There are things going on out in the big world. I want to get on with them."

Megan swallowed. She could just imagine what Wilma's reaction to this news was going to be. "Burt, doing just *what?* It would make me feel a lot better if I had some idea what you were getting into."

He and Bodo glanced at each other again. "I can't get into it, Megan," Burt said. "I promised I wouldn't."

"Promised *who?*"

Burt sat down by the stream on one of a number of boulders that might have been dropped there by some ancient glacier, if this landscape had been real. "Look . . . I can't get into it, that's all. It's like I told Wilma—and even then, maybe I was saying too much. I've found out about some really interesting work I can be doing, and I'm going to go start doing it in the next few days, if everything works out all right."

"Just where did you find out about this?"

"Oh, there are a lot of little nooks and crannies in this virtual environment," Bodo said, smiling slightly. "Including some that the Breathing Space people don't know about."

Megan looked at him dubiously. "Come on, Megan, don't act so shocked," Burt said. "Is there a single virtual space on this planet that *hasn't* been compromised at some point or another? Or bent into some new shape by the people who used it, some shape that the builders never imagined? Heck, you can make a case for the idea that the whole old Internet system grew out of the machinations of ten or twenty people who wanted to use their college computers to play starship shoot-'em-up games with other students a thousand miles away. Definitely not what those first network designers had in mind for their machines! This is just more of that kind of thing."

"Goes on all the time," Bodo said, glancing around him. "This place is full of holes. Some of them were left there accidentally by the programmers. . . . They were good, but they weren't omnipotent. Others . . ." He smiled a secretive smile.

"Others were made, you're saying," Megan said. "By someone from outside."

"Not always," Bodo said. "Some of them were drilled out from the inside. For one thing, there's more than one way in and out of here."

Megan raised her eyebrows, trying to conceal how worried she was feeling. "That's not what they say."

"Shows what 'they' know," Bodo said. "But there's always a back door . . . that's what the programmers say. With a little practice, a little ingenuity, you can always find one."

"But why?" Megan said. "If the whole point of this place is protecting the kids using it—"

"Oh, yeah, it's good for that," Burt said. "No one's going to deny it. But at the same time, sometimes things can get a little . . . stifling. You know? All the counselors, monitoring your every word to see if you're coming along . . . Oh, of *course* they do, Megan, it's in the contract, we all know it. It's the one tradeoff they do require, a little. Privacy for safety."

"And sometimes," Bodo said, "some of us find a way around it. Not obviously, mind you. But there are little pockets in this system that its sysops and programmers don't know about, and some of us have found ways to exploit them. 'Quiet' spots, like the reverse of the whispering spots under a dome—places where you can't be heard. This is one of them. . . . Or else people devise ways to get 'out' into the Net without the monitors catching us and monitoring what we do or where we go."

He smiled. It was an unusually angelic smile from someone whose looks proclaimed him as being on the outer edge of things, or at least headed that way.

"It's like in the old days," Burt said, "and like it is now. If you can't meet other kids your age at home without being eavesdropped on, you go out and meet them on the corner. There are little 'street corners' here and there, scattered around Breathing Space . . ." He swallowed, for once looking just faintly nervous. "Megan, look, I can't go into a lot of details," Burt said. "But the door swings both ways. There are people who know about the street corners . . . and they meet you there and talk business. It's good business, and it pays enough to be interesting. It's nothing dangerous, nothing illegal. And that's all I'm going to say about it. I may have said too much as it is. . . ."

"I think you're okay," Bodo said, "but better drop it. The walls have ears around here." He looked resigned. "Come to think of it, even the *air* has ears."

Megan sat there looking around them and the deceptively tranquil surroundings, her mind racing. She very much doubted that the Breathing Space administrators themselves, having gone to considerable trouble to set up a place where vulnerable kids would be safe from attack, would be in any way responsible for these covert recruitments to . . . *what?* There was no telling, and she thought it was unlikely she was going to get any more out of Burt on the matter. "So you're going to vanish all of a sudden," she said, "is that it? And I'm supposed to tell Wilma that this is all right, and there's nothing to worry about?"

Burt had the grace to look slightly guilty. "I won't just 'vanish,' " he said. "I may drop out of sight for a few days at a time. I might do that anyway, you know. We're not prisoners here, they don't try to keep us against our will. Lots of kids come and go from the physical Breathing Space facilities every day without anyone getting all upset about it."

This isn't just anyone! This is one of my best friends, and your girlfriend, if you could just bring yourself to admit it! But plainly he couldn't. Megan looked down at Burt, sitting on his rock, and said, "Burt, I think this is a really bad idea. I wish you'd reconsider."

He looked up at her with an expression that hardened as she watched it. "All my life," Burt said, "people have been telling me that my ideas were bad ones. Okay, sometimes they were. But even the *good* ones, they would claim were bad ones because they didn't agree with them. This is just more of the same."

He got up. "I'm telling you, so you can tell her. Don't worry about me. I'll be fine, and I'll come back in better shape than I left . . . a lot better."

Burt turned his back and headed off, up the slope of the next hill. Bodo glanced after him, then over at Megan. It was a surprisingly commiserating look. "I'll stay with him," he said. "As long as he lets me, anyway. He's a nice guy, even if he does kinda have a temper."

"Uh, thanks," Megan said. Bodo sketched her a little salute, and went off after Burt. She watched them vanish over the next hill—literally, 'vanish'—first Burt, invoking the optional "invisibility" that the Breathing Space provided, and then Bodo, in his wake.

Megan stood there silent for a moment or so. *He's just angry, he's taking it out on the people around him, he'll think better of it eventually and stop this kind of thing*, Megan thought.

But she doubted he'd do so very soon. Maybe that was her bad opinion of him talking. At the same time he obviously hadn't thought about the effect his actions were going to have on Wilma . . . or if he had, Burt didn't care.

I can't let this just happen. I can't. It would be like letting someone drive drunk. Anything that happens to Burt, or to anyone who gets caught up in whatever he's going to do, would be on my head . . . and I couldn't stand it afterward.

Megan turned and made her way back to the doorway to her own space. Once there, she vanished the doorway and sat down at her desk under the hard back sky of near-Saturn space, leaned on her elbows, laced her fingers together, put her chin down on her hands, and thought hard.

"Workspace manager . . ."

"Listening, Megan."

"I want all the information you can find about the history, management, and structure of the Breathing Space youth refuge facilities."

"Finding that information for you now. Limiting parameters?"

"None." It was going to land a terrible amount of information on her desk to be sifted through. But Megan had a feeling that buried somewhere in it all could be a hint of exactly what Burt was getting into, something that could help her help him . . . and she wouldn't know what it was until she saw it.

Her first and simplest impulse—to go straight to the Breathing Space people and 'blow the whistle' about what was happening—Megan had already rejected out of hand. All she had at the moment was hearsay evidence, and even though she felt certain Burt was telling her the truth, that wasn't going to count for much with the administrators of Breathing Space. She would at least need evidence of one of these "street corners," and an indication of how it worked, and she had neither. She might have to think about adapting a "mask," a false virtual identity, to see if she could find anything out that way. But that was very much a last-resort idea.

"Ready," said Megan's workspace. "Warning: material comprises the equivalent of some four thousand typed pages."

Megan smiled grimly. "Let's go."

Rhea went around Saturn at least once while Megan sat there, reading window after window of text that scrolled through the air in front of her in hanging windows, watching flat movies and stereo screenshots and full-virt interviews and pieces of documentaries play themselves out on the floor of her amphitheater. She plowed through all kinds of data; description, commentary, interviews, editorials, testimonials, even precís of court cases—for there had been quite a few of these over the years, people trying to get at their estranged kids by (for instance) claiming that the Breathing Space people had brainwashed them, or even kidnapped them. Other people had tried bribery, or even blackmail, to subvert Breathing Space staff and get them to reveal the physical locations of runaways, so that they could be snatched. The environment itself had been hacked into spectacularly once in the very early part of the century, when virtuality as people knew it now was just getting started, then it had been briefly and disastrously exploited by a ring of criminals specializing in child slavery, and worse. Since then, the Breathing Space organization had made the reorganization and security of its virtual spaces its highest priority, next to the care of the kids those spaces sheltered. The Breathing Space "sheltered environment" was now as watertight and secure as anything could be these days . . . or so it was publicly claimed.

But Bodo was right. Where there was a will to make an alternate way in, or out, someone would manage it. If hacking talent had ever been hard to acquire since computers began, it certainly wasn't now. Most kids knew a whole lot about the guts of the Net at a very early age, since so much emphasis was put on it in school, both as a learning tool and a way to help you with your homework . . . not to mention all the rest of your life. A lot of kids, like those who got seriously into simming, learned a great deal about systems analysis and how to best exploit the hardware/software interface for their own hobbies and pursuits. It wouldn't take that much time, Megan supposed, to find out a fair amount about how to subvert the kind of safeguards that Breathing Space must have around its virtual territory. *And like any guarded space,* Megan thought, *it would be most vulnerable to attack from within. From the very people it's supposed to be protecting.*

The problem is that nobody really likes to admit they need protection. She put her head down on her hands again for a moment. *It implies that you're weak. Pretty soon you're looking for ways to prove you don't need any protection after all, you can take it, you're just using this place to get a little rest . . . and meanwhile, you're bending the rules, and the system structure, so that you can do things your way.*

Control . . . it was all about control. "The great adolescent dilemma" was the phrase used by one of the editorial writers who'd experienced Breathing Space from the inside, briefly, and talked to some of the kids there. Well, maybe he was overdramatizing. But there might be something to it. No teenager Megan knew had been able to avoid moments when they thought they would just burst, or go crazy, because of pressure from parents or teachers not to assert themselves, *not* to do something unique or even slightly dangerous that they really wanted to do. The urge to get away on your own, ideally with enough money to make it pleasant, the urge to run your life . . . it seemed, sometimes, that as it got stronger and stronger with the approach of adulthood, your parents stepped on it harder and harder. Even the relatively light rein on which Megan knew her parents "rode" her sometimes irked her out of all proportion to the actual control. She had never left home, but there had been times when the thought had crossed her mind, all right. How much more was someone like Burt going to feel the urge . . . ?

Meanwhile, none of this solved the basic problem. What *was* this "work" that Burt was so interested in?

And why would anyone be offering kids in Breathing Space work? Though Breathing Space itself as a charitable organization was a wonderful idea, Megan very much doubted that any altruism was behind *these* offers. The world was just too full of people busy taking advantage of other people, and the fact that the approaches were being made in secret made Megan even more suspicious. Surely anyone legitimate would simply go to the environment's administrators and offer to help employ their clients when they got out. It would be wonderful publicity . . . for anyone who wanted publicity.

Well, let's try to approach this logically. Just what has Breathing Space got?

Runaways.

No, she had to be less judgmental about it. Good strategic analysis meant taking a concept apart into its smallest possible pieces, not trying to work with a large emotive whole. *Troubled kids*, Megan thought, *usually under legal age. Sometimes, people who've been declared missing persons, or are otherwise in some kind of trouble with the law.*

. . . Not exactly your optimum employees. These kids might not have a fixed address, and might not want one. They probably wouldn't have much of a work record . . . sometimes might not have documentation, or might not even be eligible to work, depending on where they are.

Now what kind of employer—

"Megan?"

She looked up at the sound of her father's voice, one of the exterior outputs for which she allowed her workspace to interrupt her. "Yeah, Dad?"

"I've already eaten lunch twice," said her father's voice, with a slight echo around it that made him sound a little like the Great and Powerful Oz. "I would do it one more time just for the heck of it, but then your mother would start calling me 'The Gut That Walks' again. So can I please have my office back?"

"Oh, jeez, sorry Dad, I forgot where I was!" Megan got up from the desk, glanced around at the litter of frames, frozen videos and virteos, and still and solid images littering the floor of her amphitheater. "Workspace manager, save everything. . . ."

"Saved." The voice then added, "This is a prescheduled reminder." And in her own voice it said, "Answer the mail, Megan, it's lying around all over the place!"

She sighed. "Later," she said. "Shut down—"

She blinked her implant off and found her father sitting in front of her and off to one side, in one of the few chairs in his office that wasn't covered with books laid out open and facedown. The sun had moved around the house, so that it was starting to come in these windows now; her father had drawn the blinds against the hot afternoon light. "Heavy session?" he said. "Or just catching up on the mail?"

"I wish," Megan said. She stretched, feeling a sudden ache in her back that hadn't been there before. "Dad, does this chair need to have its massage machinery checked?"

"They just tuned it last month, honey, when the support people came around to do the usual maintenance." He looked thoughtfully at her. "Any possibility that it's just stress?"

" 'Possibility'!" Megan said, and laughed, but there wasn't much humor in the sound.

"Anything you care to talk about?" her dad said as he sat himself down in the chair.

Megan took a deep breath, then shook her head. "Not until I know for sure what I'm talking about," she said. "Is the other machine free?"

"For a miracle, yes," her dad said. "Your brothers both decided to go out at once . . . the place has been unnaturally quiet. But, Megan, why not have some lunch first. If you're going to worry about things, there's no point in doing it on an empty stomach."

Her stomach growled emphatically. "Yeah," Megan said, "not a bad idea. . . ."

The simple fact of hunger distracted her more than Megan would have thought. Even when she was done eating a sandwich that would have astonished even Mike, she didn't much feel like going virtual again that afternoon. It was partly that Megan was conscious of spending a whole lot of her time in the Net lately, more than usual, but also an acknowledgement of a feeling of discomfort with Burt's basic problem. For all her occasional problems with her brothers and her parents, Megan was troubled by the concept of home as Burt must see it; as a place you didn't want to be, somewhere you wanted at all costs to escape from. *Maybe if I'm going to figure this out*, she thought, later that evening, while curled up with her father's immense copy of *The Complete Dickens* in a chair in the living room, *I'm going to have to try to think more like someone who doesn't see home as the center of life, the safe place. . . .* There were certainly enough people in Dickens' writing who felt that way, and Megan spent the rest of the evening immersed in *David Copperfield*, trying to get a handle on the insecurity and the pain.

The next morning was Monday morning, and for Megan, Burt's business and the matter of whatever was going on at Breathing Space retreated somewhat into the background, especially after she left a virtmail for Wilma about having seen Burt, and Wilma didn't answer it, though her system acknowledged that she'd read it. *Maybe he's been in touch with her, finally,* Megan thought. *Maybe things have gone off the boil, a little . . . Which would be good.* While the school year was fast winding down toward summer, there were still final exams to think about; in particular, the upcoming advanced-placement math final was giving her the creeps. She had been doing all right in classwork, and much to her relief had finally been getting to grips with the parts of calculus that had been eluding her, these last couple of months. But now, with the final exam only two weeks away, Megan was starting to get nervous. She left the virtmails piled up on her desk for the next couple of days, and spent practically all her free time immersed in integrals and other associated discomforts, telling herself that she would never need this junk once she was working for Net Force as a strategic operations analyst. *And when that day comes I'll toast marshmallows over my burning math books. . . .*

It was fairly late Wednesday evening when she looked up from her fourth attempt to solve one particularly knotty integral and glanced at where Saturn was in the sky. She did a quick calculation in her head. *My God, it must be eleven-thirty*, Megan thought. *Why am I still here torturing myself like this?*

She looked down at the integral on the math-workbook datapad on her desk. "Oh, go on," Megan said in annoyance, "show me the answer."

Her handwriting on the surface of the pad disappeared, to be replaced by the tidy print of the workbook program's output. Megan leaned down to look at the result, started to swear, and then stopped herself. *Too damn simple*, she thought. *Why do I always go at this stuff the complicated way? Sometimes it's genuinely easy. Why do I have trouble believing that?*

She straightened up, and at the same moment heard the sound of someone "knocking" for admission to her workspace. "Yeah?" Megan said.

Wilma stepped suddenly out of the air into her space. That surprised Megan. Wilma wasn't terribly good at staying up late. "Wil? What's up—"

But immediately, from the look on Wilma's face, Megan knew. "Have you heard from Burt at all lately?" Wilma said, urgent.

"Uh, no, not since Sunday. I've been sort of busy—"

"He's gone," Wilma said.

Megan let out a long breath. "Gone where?"

"I don't know. I tried to get in touch with him a couple of times. Monday, Tuesday . . . He was there, but he wasn't available. I left him virtmails. No answer. And then, a little while ago, I queried them again. . . ." Wilma shook her head, and her face was a study in shock, the face of someone coming to terms with something she'd been trying hard to believe wouldn't happen for a long while yet. "He took all his things this afternoon, they said, and left Breathing Space. . . ."

Megan swallowed. *Oh, God, did I make this happen sooner than it might have otherwise?* she thought, flushing first hot and then cold with fear. *So this is how you keep him from "driving drunk"? Hey, nice work.*

"Megan, what am I going to do? We've got to find him!" Wilma said.

"Yeah," Megan said. "We'll find him."

But she had no idea how. . . .

5

The rest of that evening was difficult. Megan found herself trying to reassure Wilma without actually lying to her.
Yet she couldn't even say "He'll be all right," because
she had no indication whatsoever that he *would* be. In fact,
Megan couldn't say much of anything, between just letting Wilma talk her fears out, and herself dealing with the
rush of sidelined concerns about Breathing Space and Burt
that were now washing over her, full force. When Wilma
finally headed back to her own space, after midnight, Megan sagged back in the chair behind her desk and just
stared into space for a little while, thinking about what to
do next.

"Space manager," she said finally.

"Listening, Megan."

"I want to talk to whatever administrative staff are
available at the Breathing Space Net address I accessed
Sunday."

"Working on that for you. Do you have a name to search for?"

"No. Just get me whoever's on supervisory duty for the facility where Burt Kamen was staying."

"Very well. Waiting for an answer."

Megan stood up behind the desk. A moment later she found herself looking at another desk, in a handsome office done in mauves and grays, colors she suspected had been picked for their restful qualities. Behind the desk was sitting a handsome middle-aged woman, conservatively dressed in a dark business jacket, a woman whose face reminded her a little of her mother's: high-cheekboned, with eyes slightly slanted, the skin around the eyes and mouth a little lined, but in ways that made Megan think of authority rather than age. "I'm Donna Killester," the woman said. "How can I assist you, Miss, uh, O'Malley?"

"I'm looking for my friend Burt Kamen," Megan said. "I understand he was staying with you until earlier today."

"He was," Ms. Killester said, "but I'm afraid I can't tell you anything about where he's gone. We've already had a couple of inquiries about him today, but I'm afraid I couldn't help them, either."

A couple? Interesting. Did his folks finally get off their fundaments and do something? "You *can't* tell me," Megan said, "or you *won't* tell me?"

She tried hard not to sound too challenging as she said it. Ms. Killester smiled just slightly and said, "Obviously there are confidentiality issues involved. But in this case, I mean 'can't.' Mr. Kamen didn't leave any indication of where he was going, or when he might be back, if indeed he intends to come back at all, since he didn't leave any personal effects deposited with the facility where he was staying."

"He can come back, though, if he wants to?"

"Of course he can," Ms. Killester said. "Our charter is very clear on our responsibilities to any young person who comes to us. We turn no one away unless they're chronically violent, or chronically involved in criminal activities . . . in which case other social services organizations get involved, as you might imagine."

Megan nodded. "Is there any way I could leave a message for him, in case he does come back?"

"Yes, of course. His Net access and virtmail accounts here are still active, so that friends and relatives can get in touch with him. They stay that way for a year. Or even longer, if a review indicates the extension is warranted. It's a very basic part of our service, one that's easy for us to provide, and it's not one we would cut off without good reason."

"All right." Megan thought for a moment. "Is there anything you can tell me about who else might have been in touch with him recently?"

"I'm sorry, but that would come under the heading of information we have to keep confidential."

Of course it would. "Right," Megan said. "Ms. Killester, I appreciate your help . . . thanks a lot."

"Thank *you*," Ms. Killester said. "I'm sorry not to be able to be of more help to you . . . but I appreciate your concern for your friend. Should he turn up again, of course we'll encourage him to get in touch with the people who've been trying to reach him."

"Thanks again," Megan said, and touched her desk in the spot which signaled to her workspace manager that she wanted to kill a connection. Ms. Killester vanished.

Megan sat there for a moment, considering whether "the people who've been trying to reach him" was a slip of the tongue confirming what she'd said about several attempted contacts, or just a general plural. No way to tell, she thought. *And I'm not sure whether it matters right now.*

She sat there thinking for a few moments more. "Please

restore all the research material I had in here earlier," Megan said.

"Restoring from Save."

It all appeared again, the various text sources and interviews frozen in midspeech, people in suits sitting or standing and talking earnestly. One of them was the Breathing Space founder, Richard Page, a tall handsome silver-haired man with a cultured accent. He was an immensely successful businessman who had decided to turn his "spare money" into something that would live on after him and do good, and who spent all his spare time (when not riding steeplechasers) shaking down other rich people for *their* spare money, to be applied to the same cause. Megan walked out into her space and stood there looking at him for a moment.

Then she said to her workspace, "I want another Net connection."

"Please specify."

"Contact the same Breathing Space facility I visited Sunday. I want to try to reach a client calling himself 'Bodo.' "

"Working on that for you."

She turned her back on Richard Page and looked up at the white tiers of her amphitheater, running up to the black sky. A moment later her workspace said, "The client has flagged himself as available for a limited time."

"Great. Open an access."

"Opening. Please note that this access is controlled. All access to the space is by express permission of Breathing Space Inc., and unauthorized accesses or attempts to enter or exit the space by other than officially sanctioned means will be prosecuted to the full extent of the law—"

"Yeah, I just bet they will," Megan muttered under her breath as her system read out the disclaimer. There were serious holes in this system. That was an issue that someone was going to have to raise with the Breathing Space people after this particular patch of dust settled. *Net Force*, probably, Megan thought. *When Burt has sorted himself out, I want to go have a talk with James Winters about this. . . .*

"Do you agree?"

"Yes, of course I agree, let's go!"

Her doorframe appeared in front of her, and the door part of it winked out. A low buzz of conversation came from the far side.

Megan walked through the door and found herself in a place as utterly unlike the peace and quiet of the previous "mountain" landscape as could have been imagined. Once again, though, once she was through she had to just stop and stand there and stare around her in admiration of the skill, the sheer love that some virtual-experience designer, or team of them, had lavished on this space. Megan seemed to be standing in the middle of a big broad plaza in the middle of a city, a handsome sunny space through which the occasional green tram passed, dinging in gentle reproach at some pedestrian crossing the tracks down at the plaza's far end. The gray stone paving of the central area was completely surrounded by old six-story buildings in some beautiful golden stone, with shutters at all the high windows and windowboxes with red and pink flowers spilling out of them. And it looked as if the bottom floor of every one of those buildings had a café in it, because tables and chairs spilled out in front of every one of them, well into the middle of the plaza. Hundreds of people sat there eating and drinking in the warm sunshine, and the whole place buzzed softly with their conversation, a low soft rush mirroring the sound of the river flowing by not too far away, at the bottom of the little "plateau" on which the plaza and the rest of this part of the city sat. Away in the distance, past the river and the nearer hills, a white line could be seen against the bottom of the blue, blue sky—more mountains.

Someone whistled at her from behind. Megan turned and smiled just a little, for there, near one of the cafés at this end of the plaza, was a sculpture of a giant wooden bear, and leaning against it, his arms folded, was Bodo. "Looking for somebody?" he said.

"You know who," Megan said, going over to him. She glanced around her as she came up to him.

"He's not here."

"I know that," Megan said. "That's what I want to talk about."

"I don't know where he is," Bodo said.

"That's not what I'm interested in," Megan said.

Bodo looked at her thoughtfully for a moment . . . then said, "Come on, let's sit down. It's summer here . . . you get hot standing around."

They headed toward the nearest café. "Quite a place," Megan said, looking around her.

"No one wants to be alone all the time," Bodo said. "Sometimes you want to be with people."

"How many of them are real?"

"You mean other Breathing Space refugees? Enough," Bodo said. "Some of them are worth talking to. But a lot of these are just recordings of normal people. Some of us forget what those are like, after a while. . . ."

Megan nodded. They went to an empty table, sat down. After a few moments a tall thin waiter in a white shirt with the sleeves rolled up, and black pants and a black apron, came along and paused by the table. "Gruezi," he said, nodding to them.

"Hi, there," Bodo said. "Got a Rivella?"

"Red or blue?"

"Blue."

The waiter turned to Megan. "Mademoiselle?"

"Uh, a Coke."

"Right away." He headed off again.

Megan looked at Bodo, raised her eyebrows. " 'Blue'?"

"You'll see." Bodo gazed away across the plaza.

"Bodo, look," Megan said. "You hardly know me. It's nice of you to take the time to see me, and so late in the day."

"I don't mind," Bodo said. "It's not a problem; I'm not doing anything today."

"I'm glad. . . . But, Bodo, I'm really worried about Burt . . . and his girlfriend, Wilma, is going to be frantic if she doesn't hear from him pretty soon."

"I don't know if that's likely to happen," Bodo said, sounding a little morose. "I don't know him all that well, but he was pretty eager to get out of here."

"That's what I want to talk to you about." They paused as the waiter came back with a tray, a couple of glasses, and a couple of bottles. He put down the glasses and poured their drinks. Megan's Coke looked as she had expected, but Bodo's drink wasn't blue at all. It was a pale golden color like a good ginger ale. They lifted their glasses.

"By the way, just so you know. This isn't real food," said the waiter.

Megan smiled half a smile in amusement at the statutory warning.

"Don't you get tired of saying that all day?" Bodo said.

The waiter looked at him, quizzically. "How could I? I'm a computer. Enjoy your drink." He went away, drying his hands on his apron.

Megan drank some of her Coke, and then put the glass down. "Listen, do you mind if I ask you a question?"

"Ask me, and I'll tell you if I mind."

"What brought *you* here?" Megan said.

Bodo gave her an odd look. Then he leaned on his elbows and watched the world go by for a moment before answering. "It was a custody thing," Bodo said. "My mom and dad were divorcing. It was messy, there's a lot of money involved. . . . Dad is rich from inventing and licensing a virtual-environment-managing concept. Mom has a lot of money of her own, old family money. They've spent the last couple of years fighting over which of them made the other more successful while they were married."

He took a long drink of his Rivella. "And one of the biggest prizes in the divorce was going to be me." Bodo's smile was sad. "Not that either of them particularly *wanted* me, you understand. My dad hates the way I look . . . my mom hates the way I think. But it didn't matter, because I was a prize, you see? When I was a kid, and they were still living together but not really being together, my mom and dad would fight to see who could give me the biggest present, or to get me to go on holidays with one or the other of them. Whoever got me to go with them, won. Now that they were finally divorcing, the game just changed a little, and both of them wanted to 'have' me because winning custody of me would really piss off the other one. They were just about to start their second year of fighting over me in family court when I decided I was tired of it all. I took a few things in the middle of the night, sneaked past the security systems around the house, and left for a Breathing Space facility in another country. And I've been in one or another of them ever since." He looked up, his eyes glinting with humor, but the humor had an edge to it. "This way neither of my parents gets me. Neither of them gets to spite the other one. I win . . . they lose. For once in my life."

"Oh, God, Bodo . . . I'm sorry."

"Don't be!" Bodo said. "I'm doing okay. I've put aside a little money. Enough that I can take 'holidays' from here and go other places. I stay in youth hostels and so on. . . . I look like some kid going on the Backpack Grand Tour. You know: 'See the world cheap before you get down to business.' " He chuckled. "No one looks twice at a kid in their 'transitional year,' if you go to the traditional places and do the traditional things. In six months I'll no longer be a minor in the—in my home jurisdiction. Then I can even go back home, if I want to, because my folks won't be able to fight over *me* anymore. All the rest of their 'stuff,' yeah, let them pull each other's heads off about that all they want. Their lawyers love it. And if my parents don't want me around anymore, because I've lost any value as a bargaining chip, that's okay, too. Being rich is really overrated, especially if you don't know how to use it so it does somebody some good . . . and you can meet some really nice people when you're 'poor' and on the road."

He had another drink of his Rivella, while Megan sat there and thanked whatever powers moved above her life that she had somehow escaped this kind of adolescence.

"Bodo," she said at last, "listen. This work that Burt's doing . . . what is it? I have to know."

"Why are you asking me about it?"

"Because you know. Because you've done it. Haven't you?"

His eyes rested on her for a long moment before he answered. "Burt's girlfriend," Bodo said, "if that's what she is—he's really worried about impressing her, you know?"

"I think 'Burt's girlfriend' is exactly what she is," Megan said, "though I'm not sure Burt's clear about it as yet. If he wants to impress her, it's not because she's particularly demanding or anything. But worried . . . that she definitely is."

"He's short of money, too," Bodo says. "The two conditions don't go together well . . . needing to look successful to someone, and being broke and on the street. He decided he was going to do something about it."

"Meaning he was going to do what you did."

Bodo looked at Megan.

"Tell me about it," she said.

He studied his drink for a few moments. "If you wait

around one of the 'street corners' in Breathing Space long enough," Bodo said softly, "you meet people who want small jobs done for them. They visit on and off for several days, usually, interviewing. Mostly they want packages carried places. Generally you don't inquire about what's in the packages. You get a strong feeling it might be better not to. The payment's good—real good, for such short-term work. These people slide in, ask around to see who's available, size them up . . . and make a deal. You leave the facility, make a pickup . . . make a drop somewhere else. That day a credit account that you've specified suddenly acquires a positive balance with some serious zeroes before the decimal point . . . the kind of figure you might take a year to see if you were working behind the counter in a convenience store." Bodo turned his glass around on the table.

Megan sat there looking at her Coke. "And you told him about this—"

"He *asked* me about it!" Bodo said. "Don't blame *me* for this, Megan. If he hadn't found out from me, he absolutely would have found it out from somebody else here pretty fast! It's hardly a secret. And I know what Burt's going through. It can be really hard not to have any money. They make you as comfortable as they can, here, they try to get you set up in work/study programs and that kind of thing if you're sure you can't go home . . . but those take a long time to pay off. When something presents itself that can make you good money, fast, for just a little work, you're likely to jump at it."

Megan swallowed. "Sorry," she said. "I didn't mean to sound like I was blaming you."

"Yeah, well," Bodo said. For a few moments they were both quiet, looking in different directions in the bright spring sunshine.

"How often do these 'recruiters' come through?" Megan said.

"Every few months," said Bodo. "The word in the Space goes around in a hurry. There's someone here, 'scouting . . .' And if you're interested, you go meet with them on one of the 'street corners.' Some kids get good at this line of work. They do it all the time. Some of them we don't see again. . . ."

A chill went down the back of Megan's neck, nothing to do with the wind off the river. "They never come back, you mean."

"Why should they? If the work's good, if they like it and do enough of it to buy themselves an apartment somewhere, or even a house somewhere cheap, what would be the point?"

Megan had another drink of her Coke to try to collect herself.

"Burt got lucky," Bodo said. "The first of the 'lookers' arrived just a few days ago. Must have been the night after he came in . . . something like that. I'd mentioned it to him in passing, but when he heard the word from someone else, he was hot to get involved, kept talking about what Wilma would think, how great he'd look when he turned up in his home neighborhood again, how happy it would make her that he didn't ever have to go home again. He went off to his meeting with—" Bodo waved his hand in the air, plainly not wanting to mention names. "Whoever they are. He came back saying they liked him, they were going to get back to him. I guess they did."

He had another drink of his Rivella. "I last saw him last night," Bodo said. "We're in the same facility, physically. He was packing up his stuff, not that he'd brought an awful lot with him to start with. Said he was going to be meeting someone in Ch—meeting someone nearby. And then this morning he left."

Megan swallowed, her mouth suddenly having gone dry despite the Coke. She was realizing that she had been phrasing her questions to herself about Breathing Space incorrectly. Not 'what kind of employer would hire these kids.' But instead, 'For what kind of employer would these kids be perfect?'

Someone who doesn't want people who have family ties.

Someone who wants people who are already missing . . . and wouldn't surprise anyone if they never came back.

. . . I've got to find him!

She turned the Coke bottle around and around on the table. "If I wanted to do work like this," Megan said, very softly, "who would I ask for?"

Bodo stared at her. "Oh, come on, you're not—"

"Bodo," Megan said, *"please."*

She looked him in the eye and would not look away.

Finally he glanced down at the red-and-white-checked tablecloth. "There's a guy named Vaud," Bodo said, hardly above a whisper. "At least, it's a male persona he wears when he's in here, and that's the name he uses."

"And what 'street corner' does he hang around?"

For a long time Bodo wouldn't say anything. Megan just sat there and looked at him.

After a while he looked up at her. "Do you like Burt or something?" Bodo said.

Megan strangled the first answer that tried to get out of her throat, since it would have profoundly shocked both her father and mother, as well as embarrassing her by making it plain that she even knew such expressions. "Not for myself," Megan said. "In fact, I'm a whole lot more inclined to kick him than kiss him at the moment. But I have to do this nonetheless. Probably I'll make an appointment for myself with the nearest shrink as soon as I've found him again."

"Huh." Bodo finished his Rivella, put the glass down, and then looked over his shoulder. After a moment he turned back to her. "You can get there from here," he said, "but not at this time of day. The schedule's wrong."

"When will it be right?"

Bodo shook his head.

"Come on," Megan whispered.

He stopped shaking his head . . . then said, very softly, "Give me a virtmail address for you."

"Link to workspace," Megan said.

"Active," said her workspace's management program in a distant whisper, hardly audible above the chatter and laughter of the crowd.

"Pass my virtmail address to client 'Bodo's' account."

"Done."

He nodded, then, not meeting her eyes. "I'll mail you," Bodo said.

"Thanks."

She started to get up . . . then sat down again. Bodo gave her a bemused look.

"Tell me one thing before I go," Megan said.

"Ask," he said, though again he wouldn't look at her.

"Why have you told me all this?" Megan said. "It could get you thrown out."

"I don't think so," Bodo said. "Well, maybe so, if they found out. I don't think they will. They're not nearly as all-seeing as they make themselves out to be. It's part of the place's protective coloration, the thing that keeps it from being exploited more than it is. But as for the rest of it . . ."

Bodo looked up at her, favoring her once more with that expression which had seemed so odd the first time. "Since I got here," Bodo said, "I mean the first time I got here, not this one . . . you're the first person who's asked me why I'm here, other than the professionals who *have* to ask."

Megan was startled. "Uh—"

"A lot of people here are real self-absorbed," Bodo said softly. "Interesting to run into someone who wasn't, for a change. Very interesting indeed."

Megan swallowed. "Bodo," she said, "I want to thank you. Thank you very much."

"Don't thank me until you've got reason," Bodo said. "I may not bc able to help you."

"You already have. And I thank you anyway." She turned away. "I'll be waiting to hear from you."

Megan activated the egress doorway back to her own workspace, closed it behind her. Not until the bright sunlight of that plaza was gone, replaced by the blackness of near-Saturn space, did she feel entirely safe again . . . and she had no idea why.

And then Megan stood there looking at the images still littering her amphitheater floor, all frozen in the middle of talking about Breathing Space. All that information in one place . . . but the one thing she most wanted to know about it, none of these people knew.

"Save everything," Megan said to her workspace management program, and turned her back on the images. *I need to think. But not in here. I've had enough virtuality for one day.*

"All saved, Megan."

"Good. Close down."

"This is a preprogrammed message. 'Megan, your mail is piling up enough that it's going to start perturbing Rhea's orbit if you don't *do* something about it!' "

She stopped where she was at the sound of her own voice, and her face twisted in annoyed response. Then Megan sighed. *The curse of a tidy mind . . .* "Abort shutdown," she said. "Show me the mail."

"Priority specifications?"

"None. Just open everything."

Shortly the bottom level of the amphitheater was littered with a crowd of talking images that looked like some kind of animated direct mail convention. Megan walked among them and examined each one in passing. Some of them were images of schoolmates other than Wilma, fervent announcements about softball games, desperate requests for bring-and-buy nights for one or another of the charities her class was sponsoring, schedules for group study sessions . . . Most of these Megan messages grabbed out of the air as if they were flimsy pieces of paper or cellophane, folded up, and "filed" in a cardboard box she'd conjured out of the empty air to follow her across the floor and receive them. Other messages—ads for restaurants, announcements about sales at stores in one of all too many nearby malls—she treated like the junk mail they were, plucking them out of the air, crunching them up into crinkly "paper" balls, and pitching them with great force up away from the surface of Rhea. They soared through the tenuous atmosphere without difficulty, heading in a leisurely manner toward Saturn and out of sight. Finally with her space looking a whole lot less cluttered than it had some minutes before, Megan came to the last virtmail, the one nearest the edge of her workspace, where the floor of the amphitheater ended, and the scatter of bluish methane snow began. There, slight, redheaded, and freckled, leaning on the hood of a Cadillac carved out of ice, Leif Anderson looked out at her.

Leif.

Abruptly, without warning, the idea began to grow in Megan's mind, and started turning into a plan, racing through her thought and swiftly strangling the objections she raised in the same way a vine strangles a sapling tree.

He would be perfect. Perfect.

But he'd never do it. And it wouldn't be fair to ask him. And besides—

Megan stood there for several long seconds, irresolute.

"Are you finished with these mails?" her system said.

"No," Megan said. She grabbed Leif's mail out of the air, crunched it back down into the iridescent ball-icon which it had been originally, and threw it straight up in the air, where it hovered. "Live link to sender."

"Working on that for you now."

Oh, please let him be up now, Megan thought, for it was pretty late. *Come to think of it, please let him be on this coast. Or this continent.* His folks traveled a lot, and Leif couldn't always be counted on to be in New York, especially as the summer got closer—

The amphitheater side of Megan's workspace went dark, and then a moment later began to glow blue with an eerie light. All that side of her workspace turned into a cave of ice—but not your usual cave. Here the ice was all of that particular pure clear blue that occurs only in the interiors of icebergs and glaciers. And in grottoes chiseled deep into the thick walls, many strange shapes stood—televisions and phone booths, plants and trees and people and animals, and many more cars than just the Cadillac. *Why an Edsel?* Megan found herself thinking, for there was one of those, too, back in the distance. She could clearly make out the peculiar radiator grille. The deepest recesses of this place were like a great long garage for cars of the previous century, all carved out of ice. "Leif," Megan said to the cold and echoing blueness, shaking her head, "not even *you* could make this up. This is so weird it has to be real somewhere."

"It's in the Alps," Leif said, coming out from the depths of the cave. He was wearing a parka, which seemed appropriate, considering the setting, but still made Megan laugh, because the temperature in here could be anything he liked without melting his virtual ice. "Somebody started carving these in the glacier early in the last century . . . other sculptors have added to the collection since then." He scowled at Megan a little. "Meanwhile, you sure took long enough to get back to me," Leif said, managing to sound genial and annoyed. "How busy can you have *been*? You—"

He stopped suddenly, and looked more closely at her, and his face changed. "Tell me, Megan," Leif said, "who knocked you down and walked over you? You look really strung out. What's the matter?"

She sat down on the hood of the icy Cadillac and started to tell him.

6

When Megan was finished, all Leif seemed capable of doing was staring at her in astonishment. *"Bozhe moi,"* he said finally.

Megan was shivering, and not because of the virtual ice all around. The reaction to some of the things that Bodo had said to her was finally catching up with her at the end of a long and stressful day. "They don't come back," she said to Leif, and slid off the hood of the Cadillac. "I can't get that out of my head. Leif, those kids aren't failing to come back because they've bought houses on the Riviera or retired to Florida. They're not coming back because they can't. They're in trouble, or locked up somewhere . . . or maybe even dead."

"That I could easily believe," Leif said.

"And my friend Burt is out there now, all excited, thinking he's on to a good thing," Megan said. "He'd probably kill me for saying this, since I'm hardly an expert, either, but he's not terribly experienced in 'the ways of the world.' He's kind of short on social skills. He tends to do things without thinking them through, and after he's made a mess, he doesn't seem terribly good at cleaning it up. He's no suave secret agent type. He is a prime candidate for just getting himself killed if we don't find out something about who's sent him where, and get him back!"

Leif nodded and stood there with his head down, his hands thrust into his parka's pockets, studying the icy floor. After a moment he looked up again.

"So what are you going to do?" he said. "Blow the whistle, obviously."

"With what evidence?" Megan said. "Even if Bodo was willing to talk to the cops about this, which I doubt, it'd just be his word they'd have to go on. No one would take us seriously. And as soon as the people responsible for this kind of 'recruitment' got a single whiff of what was going on, they'd be over the hills and far away. Probably no one in Breathing Space would hear from them again for months, maybe years, until the 'recruiters' figure the heat's died down. But I don't think that'll be the only thing dead by then."

Leif paced back and forth across the frost-powdered blue ice of the floor. Megan swallowed. "What we need to draw them out," she said, "is for someone to show up that the recruiters would really want to hire . . . someone they'd be absolutely crazy *not* to hire."

There was a long pause at that. "Someone, for example, who knows two or three languages," Leif said then. "Or four. Or six . . ."

He looked at her with slightly narrowed eyes, but also with amusement. The expression looked a lot older than the sixteen-year-old who wore it.

"That's why you're here, isn't it," he said.

"I would never ask you," Megan said hurriedly.

"But you'd let me figure it out for myself."

"Leif, believe me," Megan said, "at first I thought I would do it myself. But there was a weak spot in that idea. I've been in the space already, as a guest, logged in and identified as such. If one of the people responsible for this secret recruitment spotted me there now, they'd be in a position to figure out exactly what I was up to."

Leif kept pacing, and didn't say anything.

"Are you home right now?" Megan said after a moment. It was never a sure thing, with Leif. His father was the head of a multinational banking and investment firm, and since Leif was very small his dad had thought nothing of taking him out of school for a couple of weeks at a time without warning, hiring a tutor for him, and carting him halfway across the planet. It was the kind of life Megan dreamed of, but Leif sometimes seemed almost bored with it.

He nodded now, looking abstracted. "Dad's taking care of some 'home office' business with the Anderson Investments board members . . . paperwork stuff. Mom's putting together a dance workshop for the New School. I finished my 'finals' work last week, so school's done for me until the fall. This is kind of a quiet time before the usual travel craziness starts in the summer."

Leif looked up. "And the quiet's been driving me nuts," he added. "I think you've hired yourself an off-duty linguist."

Megan swallowed hard. "Leif . . . we've been in a bad spot or two before, and walked away from it. But this is different. I don't think this is going to be very safe."

"It's not going to be simple, either," Leif said. "For one thing, if I'm going to be the 'inside man,' I have to *get* inside. And it would kind of cause talk if I suddenly turned up at a genuine Breathing Space center and logged myself in as in need of a place to stay." Leif grimaced. "My dad would think we'd had some kind of breakdown in communication . . . and my mom would rip my head right off my shoulders and give it a big talking to." He shook his head. "We're going to have to 'fake' me in there somehow, under a seeming. Falsify the virtual ID 'tags' that the Breathing Space system puts on its users . . . and find a way to get into their safe virtual space without going through one of the approved gateways." He looked thoughtful.

"All very illegal . . ." Megan said.

"Sure, I know that. But on one level, how hard can it be? The 'recruiters' are plainly doing it at will. What they can do, I bet someone we know can help us do. But we can't take all day about it, either, if as your buddy Bodo says the Recruiters are only there for a few days every few months."

Megan nodded. "What I'm not exactly clear about yet," she said, "is what we're going to do when we find out who these people are."

Leif's slight smile went grim. "I wouldn't bank big money on ever finding out who they *really* are. But what they want, and how they're operating . . . that's another story. If we can spoil that here and now, we'll have done something worthwhile. The important thing is to get the access fakery sorted out. I think I might be able to get help on that today."

"Okay. But, Leif, there's another problem. We can't just toss you at the Recruiters blind. We need a script."

"I'm not ready to make the movie of my life yet," Leif said.

"I don't mean that. Besides, you're not photogenic enough. I mean we need—"

"I beg your pardon. I'm told I'm handsomer than most."

Megan rolled her eyes. "Leif, just wrap it up tight and put it *away*! Like you need to fish for compliments. I mean we need a backstory for you. Something to account for all these languages, and, dare I say it, a rather unstarved look."

Leif had the grace to blush. "I can starve if I have to."

"Yeah, well, better get started, because these people may be a little suspicious if you look absolutely in the pink of health. Why would someone with your good looks and talent be on the road all of a sudden? And why can't you produce any ID at all? Why isn't there any previous evidence of you in the Net?"

"There's plenty of evidence."

"All of it about Leif, not about this nameless kid who turns up all of a sudden looking good and speaking six or nine or thirteen languages! You've got to convince me that you're not a plant."

"I *am* a plant."

"You're so helpful. Don't make me start making unkind remarks about the vegetable kingdom. Start making up a story about yourself that'll hold water."

He grinned at her. "All right . . . I should be able to come up with something in time. Once I've got that handled, and we've seen what can be done about the 'fakery,' when do you want to meet?"

"The sooner the better, probably," Megan said. "I'm waiting for a virtmail from Bodo, but I have no idea when it'll come."

"You're not concerned about *if* it'll come . . ."

She thought of Bodo's odd look at her. "No," Megan said. "He'll mail, one way or another."

"Okay. Time for me to get busy, then. You go get some sleep. . . . You look like you could use it. I'll call you in the morning. You have class tomorrow?"

"Unfortunately, yes," Megan said.

"When do you leave?"

"About quarter of eight."

"I'll be in touch with you around seven, then. That okay?"

She nodded, glanced back toward her doorway. "Leif," Megan said slowly, "it's a lot to ask of you, getting involved with this. I feel guilty already."

Leif leaned against the chilly Cadillac again, dusting at the right front "headlight" with one sleeve of his parka, and then looked up at her. "What do you want me to say," he said, "that I wouldn't do it just because you asked? Well, I wouldn't." He grinned at her shocked expression. "Sorry, I couldn't resist. But first of all, it's not like you're asking me something you wouldn't have been willing to do yourself. But also, this isn't just about your friend, is it? Looks like there could've been a lot of kids our age . . . younger, even . . . who these people have used. Putting a stop to that seems like a good thing to be involved with. And as I said, I don't have anything better to do for a couple of weeks, until my dad gets his head out of the corporate filing cabinet and my mom stops speaking in dance notation twenty hours a day. So don't bother feeling guilty about anything. Let's get on with business and make your plan happen."

Megan nodded and made her way toward the doorway back into her workspace . . . then paused, turned. "Leif?"

"You still here?"

She laughed at his gibe. He could be infuriating sometimes . . . but it was worth putting up with.

"Thanks."

"You're welcome. Now go away so I can start thinking about my new 'life.' "

Megan went.

In the old Union Station in Chicago, Burt stood near a magazine stand by the foot of one of several flights of stairs leading down into the white-marble main waiting room. As far as he was concerned, the place was earning its name: he was waiting, as he had been for several hours now. Burt was bored out of his mind, and he leaned there

looking one more time at the statuary group over the big
old door opposite him, surrounding the big station clock.
The figures leaning on the clock were (he supposed) intended to represent Day and Night. He could understand
why Day was holding, in his hand, a rooster. What was
less clear was why Night appeared to be holding a penguin.

It was the kind of thing, Burt thought, that would have
driven Wilma crazy. She tended to be very structured
about everything. Everything had to make sense. She
wanted everyone around her to know his or her role and
stay in it. The trouble only started when you tried to slip
out of one role into another.

Burt was getting ready to do that . . . though he had
only recently started putting it to himself just that way.
Since he had actually left home, it had become plain to
him that he was going to have to make things work, now,
was going to have to make a success of this new life.
Otherwise his parents, if they found out he had somehow
messed it up, would never cut him a moment's slack for
the rest of his life. If everything went well, there would
be a day when Burt would go back to them and magnan-
imously offer to take them back into his life, even after
the way they had treated him. He was counting on his
father to refuse, and after that he would be, for the first
time in his life, completely free. But first Burt had to get
on his feet and start making some kind of living. And if
he was ever realistically going to ask Wilma to share that
life with him—a request he had been trying to figure out
how to make, sometime in the next few years—he was
going to have to be able to support her. Burt knew that
some people these days would consider that kind of thinking old-fashioned . . . but it was just the way he was.

That concept had been very much on Burt's mind when
he had first met the man called Vaud, the man Bodo and
some of the others had said was the one to talk to, on the

"street corner"—which looked nothing like a street corner at all, but was just a blank blue-swirled little pocket of virtual space off a city plaza that Burt hadn't recognized. The pocket into which Burt had stepped from a nondescript doorway in the plaza contained a table, a couple of chairs, and Vaud, a salt-and-pepper-haired man sitting there in a dark suit with his hands folded, on one side of the table. There was no telling what he *really* looked like, of course; as in most virtual environments, anybody could look like anything they felt like, and this man probably had reasons to want to keep his identity private, considering the kind of work he was offering. He was a short man, but there was no sense of him being small. Everything about him suggested power and control. He had turned on Burt a sharp, narrow, cool-eyed regard, when they were introduced, and questioned him closely about what he thought he was going to get out of this job. "The money," Burt said, and that cool face produced just a crack of a smile, the kind of crack you might get in a stone wall—somewhat intimidating with its suggestion that it might possibly split wider, with unfortunate results. Burt told Vaud the truth. His mother and father were not looking for him, he had no intention of going home any time soon, and that they knew this, that his friends weren't concerned enough about him to come looking for him— they knew he could take care of himself. All this the man called Vaud had listened to without much comment. Burt had shown him his driver's license when asked. It was clean, no points—but then there hadn't been time to get many, especially with his father unwilling to let him drive the car much farther than the local shopping center.

"What can you do?" Vaud said to him finally.

"Keep my mouth shut," Burt said firmly.

Vaud's smile widened, another crack in the wall, an alarming look. Burt didn't react, for what he had said was true enough. He had had endless education in that particular art from his father, who would tell him to shut his mouth about once every half-hour. But Burt also meant the phrase as he strongly suspected Vaud meant it. He would work and not ask questions, and not discuss it with anyone. Doubtless that suited Vaud's needs, but it also suited Burt's. He didn't really feel like discussing, with Wilma or anyone else, where he was going to be getting the money he was about to start making. He preferred to keep its source mysterious, if only because his life had always been short of mystery, and now that he had the chance to insert some, he intended to do just that.

"That'll do," Vaud had said at last, and told Burt to go on. If he was going to be considered for hiring, Vaud would message him the next day. Burt had gone out into that big busy plaza pretty sure that he had blown it. But the next day the message had come through, and then had come the meeting with the two other people, men—they might have been men—who were never identified to him. The one who wore the black sliktite, a tall young man whose face somehow always managed to be in shadow, even in that evenly lit place, never spoke the whole time. The other, a little round man who wore a suit like Vaud's and a face that could have been cheerful if anything like a smile ever got near it, let Vaud ask all the same questions again. Burt answered them doggedly, with no trace of annoyance at having to repeat himself. And finally, when the three looked at one another and then exchanged nods, Burt could have whooped for joy, but restrained himself.

"We'll try you out," said the little round man. "A little package needs to be picked up in Chicago and taken to Amsterdam. The people you meet there will have one for you to bring back. They'll give you instructions on where it has to be delivered."

"All right," Burt had said.

And now here he was, on time. He was mostly de-

lighted with the way things were going. He had an overnight bag. He had in his wallet, for the first time in his
life, the photo-embossed plastic card that was his passport—produced for him, by methods he hadn't inquired
into, and forwarded to him, the day after he had agreed
to take this job. His things, removed from Breathing
Space this morning, were now in a left-luggage facility at
O'Hare, and there they would stay for at least several
days. Everything was going well, and Burt was in high
spirits . . . but there was one thing very wrong. The man
he had been sent here to meet, the one making the delivery
of the package intended for Amsterdam, was very late.
Was this some kind of test, to see if Burt had enough
patience? Or was it just an accident? No telling. Burt
waited. He had a magazine rolled up under his arm, but
he had read it three times now. He let his eyes rest again
on Day and Night, and once again wondered about the
penguin. . . .

Until he saw the hat. He had seen Shriner's headgear
before, on occasion, when he was young. Now he saw
one all bright with gaudy embroidery across the lines of
polished wood benches in the waiting room, on the head
of a man who had to be about six feet six, a man booming
out jovial laughter at something a shorter man walking
next to him had just said. They paused together in the
aisle between the rows of benches, looking up at the clock
and checking their watches.

And after that it all happened very fast. The man in the
Shriner's fez—and very strange it looked, contrasted with
the ordinary business suit—came wandering over to the
magazine stand, and put down his own overnight bag next
to Burt's. He browsed the magazines for a moment,
bought a copy of *Field and Stream*, and bent down to
pick up his bag again, looking at the cover. Then he
strolled off to rejoin his friend, and the two of them van-

ished out one of the side doors, toward the corridor that led to the suburban trains.

Except that he was carrying Burt's bag, and had left his own.

After a little while, as the clock chimed the quarter-hour, Burt picked up the bag and slung it over his shoulder, unzipping the top of it to put his magazine away. As he did, he saw inside it the yellow jiffy-bag which he had been told to expect.

And that's all there is to it. . . .

He let out a long breath. This was it at last, the real start of the change in his life—the change that in a few years would see him and Wilma settled down, safely past the discomfort and mutual misunderstandings that seemed to be getting into things at the moment. They would get married, and buy a house, and start a family . . . one that would be nothing, nothing at *all*, like the one Burt had grown up in.

But that would come later. Right now, time to leave. He had an hour before the check-in time for his flight.

But Burt did one last thing before he left the station. Casually he walked to that far door, over which the big clock was mounted, and had a good long look up at it. The door itself was impassable now, walled up with marble that matched the walls. This seemed to have been done in the last century, maybe during a renovation of the station. But Burt's attention was elsewhere. From right underneath the clock, he could see that the sleepy-faced statue of Night was holding, not a penguin, but an owl. It appeared, though, to be an owl carved by someone who had never seen one before, which explained its rather strange shape.

Burt sighed. *Funny*, he thought, *I kind of liked it better as a penguin. I bet Wil would have liked it, too. . . .*

Smiling, Burt headed out of the station, making his way to the Metro line that went to the airport. It was going to be a long flight to Amsterdam, and he was planning to enjoy every minute of it.

7

Megan woke up earlier than she normally would have, even after the talk with Leif. Her anxiety wouldn't let her sleep. As a result, she found her mother in the act of getting ready to leave for the airport—heading off for some meeting in New York that couldn't be conducted virtually. Megan often wondered what went on at these, for whatever else seemed to be going on at work, the *Time* staff seemed to go out of their way to get together physically once a month for the "screaming sessions" her father had mentioned to her in passing. Her mother always came back from these meetings looking energized and cheerful, almost younger than she had when she'd left; but on the mornings of departure she was always grim, and she barely looked up when Megan came into the kitchen in a desperate search for caffeine.

"I hate these early mornings," her mother said to the air. "I went freelance to *avoid* these early mornings. I am

supposedly still freelance. Why, then, does it appear to be
five-thirty in the morning?"

"Six," Megan said. "The Earth rotates, Mom."

"Six! Oh, heavens, where's the cab?"

"It'll be here, Mom," Megan said, putting the heat on
under the kettle. "By now Kevin knows better than to be
late."

"But what if they don't send Kevin?"

The kettle started whistling almost immediately. Meg
made tea and watched her mother take what appeared to
be the third or fourth inventory of her coat and briefcase.
As she straightened up from this, someone honked outside
the house, and Meg's mother grabbed coat and briefcase
and headed for the door.

"Whoa!" Meg said, picked up her mother's reading
glasses from the table, slapped them into their case and
handed them to her mother.

"I hate this," her mom said. "Hate it. Remind me to
resign."

"Resign, Mom."

"Right. Bye bye, honey, have a good day. Better than
mine, I hope."

"Bye-bye, Mom. You'll feel better in a while."

"From your mouth to the Deity's ear, daughter of
mine," her mother said, heading out the door.

"Tear 'em a new one, Mom!" called a voice from the
front door.

"Arrrgh," Megan heard her mother say as she got into
the cab. Chuckling, Megan closed the side door, hearing
Mike do the same at the front.

She got some sugar for her tea, then went into the den
and settled herself in the implant chair. A few moments
later she was standing by her desk in her workspace, holding the mug of tea and looking around to see if there were
any new virtmails. *Nothing. Damn. Suppose he doesn't
. . . Suppose he changes his mind. . . .*

But there was no point in worrying about it right now. "Manager . . ." she said to her workspace.

"Here, Megan."

"Link to Leif Anderson's space."

"That link is already active. He has been waiting for you." The doorframe appeared on the floor of her amphitheater. "Please go through."

Megan went through into the ice cave. It was brighter. The earlier lighting must have been twilight, she thought. As she stood there, looking around her, a figure moved in the depths of the cave, down by the ice-Edsel, and came toward her.

It was Leif . . . she thought. He looked pallid and worn. His hair, normally a surprisingly fiery red, looked dull and tired. He looked thin, and there were shadows under his eyes. Even his skin tone looked bad—it looked *looser* than usual, somehow. Megan sucked in breath. "Leif? Are you sick, are you coming down with something? What's *happened* to you?"

He grinned at her and straightened up. "Makeup," Leif said. "If anyone wants to meet me in the nonvirtual mode, I don't have to be afraid of looking too good."

"Boy, you're right about that," Megan said. "You look like death warmed over."

"Good," Leif said. "Naturally, in Breathing Space, I'll wear a seeming that matches this one fairly closely. It might look a little better, to maintain the illusion. . . . Most people who look this bad would try to improve their looks a little while virtual. But out in the real world, this'll fool a surprising number of people. My mom's taught me a lot about stage makeup . . . and even in broad daylight, there's a lot you can get away with if you really know your own skin tone."

"If you were unscrupulous," Megan said, admiring, "you could get off a lot of school that way."

"Don't remind me. There have been times . . ."

There was a soft chime in the depths of the ice cave. "Come on in!" Leif said.

A slight young dark-haired boy with slightly Asian features walked out of the air and glanced over at them. "Hey, Megan."

"Mark!" Mark Gridley was small, and fairly young for a Net Force Explorer. But he was also one of the sharpest and most devious young minds that Megan had ever had the dubious pleasure of being associated with . . . besides being the son of Jay Gridley, the head of Net Force. There was very little that Mark couldn't get a Net-oriented computer, facility, or resource to do if he was properly motivated, and Mark didn't take much motivating, being possessed of a curiosity that would have made the Elephant's Child look like an ostrich by comparison. Megan often reflected that it was a good thing Mark was on the side of law and order. Otherwise, the law enforcement organizations responsible for online life, meaning Net Force in particular, would have their work cut out for them. *Far better he should be used for "peaceful purposes . . ."*

"Took you a while," Leif said.

"I was busy," Mark said, sounding mournful. "It's harder than usual getting online time when we're traveling."

They glanced at the dim and hazy background out of which he'd walked, a sort of swirling default blue. "Where are you, exactly?"

"Paris," Mark said, making it sound more like he might as well have said "Alcatraz." "Boy, am I glad it's lunchtime here. I'd hate to get up as early as you two."

"Go on, rub it in some more," Megan said. "What've you been doing over there? Is it a vacation?"

"Don't I wish," Mark said. "Why does my dad have to go do these things physically? He could be there in a second, virtually, and not mess up my work schedule." Mark sighed. "But he feels the need to go 'press the flesh' sometimes. Claims he can tell things from actually being with people that he can't tell just from virtual experience. And he insists on bringing me along to 'expand my horizons.' He can't fool me . . . he's just trying to keep me out of trouble. Unsuccessfully, I might add, since here I am." Mark grinned innocently. "He has to take his Net hardware with him wherever he goes . . . but at least he isn't always using it. I can get *some* business done."

Megan reflected that Mark must be one of the few human beings on the planet who could be taken out of school and sent on an all-expenses-paid vacation to Europe and still feel like he was being badly treated. "So this is what you meant when you said you thought you knew someone who could manage the 'fakery,' " Megan said to Leif. "I see your point. Mark, what have you got?"

"Well. I won't bore you with the technical details—"

Leif and Megan exchanged skeptical looks.

"Come on, you guys, eventually you have to learn *something* about the bones of the system you use every day—"

"Not today, we don't," Megan said.

Mark sighed like a philosopher denied the chance to cast pearls before swine. "Well, after Leif called me and told me what you told him, and what you two were thinking of, I went and had a look at Breathing Space's security 'cordon.' It's comprehensive, but not watertight . . . but then no system is watertight, if you poke it hard enough." Mark frowned. "The problem is, I didn't have to poke it *nearly* hard enough."

"You didn't?" This surprised Megan a great deal, after what she had read about the hacking attacks on Breathing Space in its early days, and the huge amounts of money the service had spent on security thereafter.

Mark shook his head. "There are entirely too many holes in their system," he said. "They're not all obvious. But there are a whole lot of side doors and back doors in and out of the space for administrative use, and someone's gotten a little careless about closing them down behind counselors and staff who've left the charity. In particular, there are even some 'ready-made' side doors, templates, sitting around stored away for assignment to new staff."

"You're kidding," Leif said.

Mark shook his head again. "This," he said, reaching into his pocket and flipping something small and bright and shining to Leif, "is one of them."

Leif caught it. It looked like an ordinary old-fashioned house key, the kind that would go into a physical lock. Megan peered over at it as Leif turned it over in his hands, and found that it even said "YALE" on it.

Mark said. "That's a symbol for one of about twenty template mail and space accounts they had lying around. A sign that someone over there really hasn't thought things through. Not in the charity itself. They don't handle their programming, it's contracted out. I know who the contractors are, too. They even do some work for Net Force. But if they did this kind of work for *our* people, and someone caught them at it, they and their contract would get flung right over the horizon. They may have implemented these 'ready-made' keys as a courtesy to the staff, or the staff may even have asked them to make them as a way to avoid extra 'call-out' charges when new entry/ exit protocols for added staff had to be written. But either way, in terms of security, it's a dumb idea. And it's entirely possible that the kids inside, the ones who're savvy to security structures, have found out about these keys, hijacked a couple of them, and are using them to set up these 'street corners' inside the main system."

Megan looked at Leif. "You don't suppose that someone on the inside has just . . . you know, let these loopholes *be* there. . . ."

Leif looked thoughtful. "Without evidence, it's hard to say. But it makes me wonder. If I was one of the people doing this shady recruiting we're interested in . . .

wouldn't it be simple to bribe someone to leave a back door or two open? Or not even anything that obvious. Just a little money slipped into someone's personal account to allow some information about Breathing Space's security structures to fall into the hands of the kids themselves, the ones inside, the ones who really want to 'tunnel out.' That way, when you come in through the same tunnel, you don't look responsible for anything in particular. . . ."

Megan thought about it. If Leif was right about this, the cynicism behind the strategy just about took her breath away.

"As far as the rest of your little plan goes," Mark said, "the way Breathing Space itself is structured is going to work in your favor. They don't revoke their clients' access to their virtual space for ninety days, in case they have second thoughts about meeting with staff or their families. So part of your backstory can be that you were in one of their facilities recently, but you came out . . . and now you're 'visiting' again."

"You're going to have to plant records that make it look like he actually was in one of them," Megan said.

Mark nodded. "Doable," he said. "I need to get the details from you first, though," he said, glancing over at Leif.

Leif grinned. "I've been assembling a precís," he said. "Some baby pictures of mine, altered just a little, in case we need them. Enough truth so that if I get asked for details, the lies will sound genuine. Enough manufactured stuff so that they won't be able to link anything to the real me."

"Send it over to my space," Mark said, "and I'll see that it gets where it's needed. The filing system in the Breathing Space mainframes has better security than the virtual space does, believe it or not. But I can crack it, given an hour or two. Which I've got," Mark said with a heavy sigh. "My dad's left me in the hotel with some of his staff, and I don't find them any more interesting than they find me."

"What hotel?" Leif said, suddenly sounding interested.

"The George V."

"Holy cow, Mark, don't just stand there, *call room service and order stuff!*"

"Why? Is the food good here?"

Leif hid his face in his hands and moaned. "You'll ruin your makeup," Megan warned him. "Cut it out. Mark, go do what you have to with Leif's files. We don't know when the word is going to come from Bodo, but I want to be ready."

"Okay," Mark said, and turned back the way he came. "What should I order? Caviar? I hate caviar."

"You've got a sweet tooth, haven't you? Have them come up and do the crêpes suzette for you. But don't let them set the curtains on fire."

"Think that's a possibility?" Mark said, his eyes glinting with interest. "I'll try it and tell you what happens."

He vanished. Megan smiled a little, but the smile came off as she looked back at Leif.

"Are you still sure about this?" she said. "I meant what I said before. This is looking less and less safe . . . and there are a lot of things that could go wrong."

"I'm sure," Leif said, surprisingly gently. "This is going to be worth doing, Megan. Now, go on. You're going to have to leave for school pretty soon."

Sighing, she nodded, and headed back for her own space.

When Megan got home from school, the first thing she did was head into the den. Mike was just settling into the Net chair. Megan came up behind him and said, "Give me five minutes."

"Go 'way, Megan, you bother me."

She leaned around him and looked into his face, and

batted her eyelashes a couple of times. "Your birthday," she said, "is getting awfully close. . . ."

Mike looked at her, and then laughed. "Five minutes," he said, and got up. "I'll go have a snack."

Megan sighed as she sat down. She had been thinking about that herself, but her guess was that when she got into the kitchen, it would look like the aftermath of Sherman's march on Atlanta, as far as food was concerned. She closed her eyes in resignation and blinked herself into her space.

Night hung over Rhea as usual. Even the Sun's full light on the rocks and methane snow never did more than make it seem like a particularly bright night, lit by a star a couple of times brighter than a full moon. Megan checked the space around her desk.

Her appetite deserted her. There was a virtmail hanging over her desk, bobbing up and down with unusual energy. It had the number 1 on it, like one of the balls that might come out of one of the old lottery machines, but in this case it meant the message was a "read-once," sent by some anonymous user from a public access and without the usual routing headers that would reveal its source. Megan hadn't seen many of these, and she was sure she knew who had sent it to her. She went over to it, poked it.

Bodo was standing there looking at her. "Tonight," he said. "Twenty hundred your time."

He vanished; the mail destroyed itself, popping like a soap bubble, and was gone.

Megan took a deep breath and called Leif.

Leif Anderson had learned very young how to be comfortable in strange and potentially intimidating places. Since he was almost big enough to walk, he never knew where he might suddenly find himself walking: down the Ginza in Tokyo or along a dirt track in Lesotho, down a

beach near Rio de Janeiro or along a pathway by the River
Thames, in the shadow of Big Ben. Leif had very early
become used to the absolute ease that his father's wealth
lent someone who wanted to get around, and during his
childhood he had learned not to take any particular notice
of it, moving gracefully and without too much fuss from
the upper east side of Manhattan to the west side of Zurich. Later, as he grew into his teens and became clearer
about how very many other people didn't enjoy such ease,
he had a brief period of discomfort with his father's
wealth and others' needs, and for a while he walked
through the beautiful and exclusive places his father took
him with a faint aura of guilt, aware that he had done
nothing to deserve such good fortune. Now, though, late
in his teens, Leif had realized that he was stuck with his
upbringing, and it was his job to make the most of the
advantages which had been showered on him; to try to
make them pay off for the people around him.

The constant movement among continents had left him
with what might have started out as a gift for languages,
but rapidly turned into just another way to exercise a
broad-ranging curiosity about everything that crossed his
path. It was hard to ask people questions all day unless
you spoke their language, so, when he was very young,
Leif started learning how to do that. He was sixteen now,
and there were very few languages on Earth that he didn't
at least know about. He spoke at least the most important
words and phrases in nearly fifty of them now—"please,"
"thank you," "Can I have the menu?" "Where are the
toilets?" and "Can I help?" Other languages he knew
much better, speaking them fluently, but he spoke them
best when in the right places, a given language's home.
He was in one of them now.

Leif looked around him from the little table where he
sat in the plaza, and grinned slightly, for he had been here
before, more than once—no way to avoid it, when your

father was involved in investment banking. This was the Bärenplatz in Bern, that city of elegant arcaded buildings six centuries old, of the Bundesrat, the Swiss Confederation's parliamentary body, and of many, many discreetly camouflaged banks, innocent behind mirrored plate glass or behind goldstone facades which revealed nothing but lace curtains and the inevitable windowboxes full of downspilling red geraniums. Those who thought all the big Swiss banks were in Zurich were deluding themselves. In quieter places, like this one and innocent-looking little Zug halfway across the country, much more serious money was stored than lay even under the pavement of the Bahnhofstrasse, for money these days came in many more concentrated forms than gold.

Leif had sat here often enough before, killing a soft drink in the sunshine and listening to the trams go by, while his father sat upstairs in one or another of these graceful old buildings, discussing money in amounts with so many zeroes after them that they didn't seem real. Off to one side, the noble squared green-bronze dome of the Bundesrat building looked down on the revelry, which this time of year never seemed to really die down. Leif could remember at least one warm night in one of the local hotels when the endless mutter and growl of conversation in the plaza had gone on until past three in the morning, causing his father to finally stick his head out the French doors and yell, "Don't you people have *homes* to go to?"

He smiled at the memory. But this time his father was nowhere in the neighborhood. This time Leif was on his own, and there was something lying in wait here that was more dangerous than any number of investment bankers.

And the chill went down his back as, in this genial reality, he felt a door open behind him, a door in the air, and someone said in a gentle accent that sounded more

Czech than anything else: "I am ready for you now, Mr. Dawson."

Leif got up and turned, and saw the blueness behind him through the doorway. No one else saw it. No one else near him was real. . . . They were all generated by the virtual environment program, as background, atmosphere, noise. *I could vanish right now, and no one would know*, Leif thought, and the thought gave him another chill. There was no consolation in the idea that Breathing Space was supervising this virtual environment. Mark had been able to subvert it without an incredible amount of trouble. What he could do, others could do. *Had* done. And there was no telling what else they knew how to do that wasn't terribly obvious right now.

Leif got up and followed the voice into the blueness. Waiting for him, as the door closed, he found a table with a chair on either side of it, and a man sitting in one of them: short, salt-and-pepper-haired, with a narrow face and a hard mouth, with gray eyes set close together and very small, fine hands laced together casually as they rested on the tabletop. The man's suit harked back to the turn of the century, as if he had found a style he liked and didn't intend to change it on account of something so ephemeral as fashion.

Leif kept his face straight and his affect flat. *"Gruezi,"* he said. Sometimes it would have been a matter of showing off to speak German so perfectly in the local dialect, but Bernerdeutsch was as idiosyncratic a form of Swiss German as any of the other forty or fifty kinds scattered around the country, and an ability to speak it well meant not only that the person speaking was linguistically talented, but that they were better than usual at blending in.

The man with the cool thin face looked at him with only mild surprise. *"Gruezi.* You may call me Mr. Vaud. Are you local?" he said, speaking formal German, *Hochdeutsch*.

"No," Leif said, "I live . . . I lived in New York. I just don't like to stand out."

"And when you go south," said Vaud, "what language do you speak down there?"

"Chei lai sudet?" said Leif, for Romansch was spoken in the southeastern cantons. *"Perei la sojourna da Italia?"* And switching languages again, *"Meish al-neimah suv uurneh."*

Vaud laughed softly. "Young man, you've never been to Morocco!" he said.

"You don't have to be," Leif said, "to speak a little of the language."

"European languages, any?"

"Spanish and Swedish I'm fluent in," Leif said, taking care to sound sullen. "Russian, too. Enough French, German, Italian, and Danish to get by. Flemish, a little."

Vaud sat there in silence for a little while and considered him. "Unusual talents for one so young."

"Don't make the mistake everyone else does," Leif said. "I'm a machine."

Just for the moment, Vaud looked confused. "You look human enough."

"I'm a performing animal," Leif said, spitting the words out with some force. "My father was a language teacher. He's been using me to experiment on for years. I'm his hobby. I never had a day of my life that wasn't full of rules and grammar and exercises. He drilled me until I was perfect at everything but saying what I really thought of what he was doing to me. Finally I got tired of being hit for mishandling the optative." Leif turned his head away. "He can sit home and do it to my little sister now, if he likes, but I've had enough of it. Meanwhile, if I'm stuck being good with languages, fine. I might as well make some money out of it."

"And your father is where?"

"Like I care."

"I ask for information's sake."

"New York. He teaches at Berlitz."

Vaud looked at the table, as if reading something there that Leif couldn't see. "And you do not foresee a reunion with him in the near future."

Leif laughed hollowly. "Boy, do I not."

"Your mother?"

"She died when I was six. I think she couldn't stand it, either—life with him, I mean. They took her to the hospital suddenly one afternoon. They told me it was a heart attack, but I knew about her sleeping pills. There were a lot of them missing afterward."

"My sympathies," Vaud said smoothly enough, though it seemed obvious to Leif that they were elsewhere. *"Dalana hewi m-iet rhunnet?"*

Leif cocked his head, then shook it. "I don't have any of the Native American languages, sorry. My dad never cared about those. He said the orthographies were too artificial." Leif made a face.

"As regards that he may have had a point," Vaud said, "but it makes little odds to us. So, *Meliankele nou moustei rhev'emien?*"

"Kai ton emen," Leif said, correcting Vaud's pronunciation. If he was going to use an idiom that had been forged on Crete, he might as well say the word the way the Cretans said it.

Vaud raised his eyebrows and spoke another phrase, this time in what Leif recognized as Tagalog, but couldn't otherwise understand. He answered in Filipino pidgin. It went on that way for about half an hour, leaving the more esoteric languages and getting into considerable detail in Russian and French, before Vaud finally sat back in his chair and looked down at the table one more time.

After a moment he said, "I take it from the fact that you sought and came to this interview in the first place that you would not be averse to doing some work on the outside."

"This place is boring me stiff," Leif said. "And the counselors are beginning to get on my nerves. Out would be good . . . and something to do that wasn't school would be good, too."

"Your talents," Vaud said, "seem considerable. There is a possibility we could use someone like you. Naturally, I must consult my colleagues in this regard, and they will want to look you over."

"Who's running this business," Leif said, "you or them?"

Vaud's lips, if possible, drew into an even thinner line than they had been manifesting already. "We are a co-operative venture," he said, "and my colleagues have a right to voice their opinions. Can you be here around this time tomorrow?"

Leif thought about it for a moment. "I don't see why not."

"I would prefer a more concrete commitment," Vaud said; the tone of voice was soft enough, but the look was sharp. "If your father has treated you harshly, that is some cause for regret, I grant you. But there is no reason to be less than civil or forthcoming with those who seek to treat you less harshly, indeed who seek to put your talents to some use."

Leif considered it time to show a little nervousness. He swallowed. "I'll be there."

"Very good. Be prompt." He glanced behind Leif, and the featureless blueness that had been swirling around him now parted to show the sunshine on the Barenplatz again.

"Good day, Mr. Dawson."

"Bye," Leif said, and went out the door. It closed behind him.

He exited from the Breathing Space virtual environment, waited for the header-strippers and other anonymizing functions that Mark had attached to his virtual persona to undo themselves, and then glanced around him. The ice cave looked a little dim. It was a function of some of the filters and protections Mark had applied to it to make sure that no one at Vaud's end of things could tell that Leif was coming in through anything but a certified Breathing Space connection.

Abruptly the dimness cleared away, and Megan and Mark were standing there, looking at Leif. "Did you get it?" he said to Mark.

"It's all down in memory," Mark said, "in triplicate."

"You said you were going to try to run a trace on that guy while the interview was going on," Megan said. "Any luck with that?"

Mark shook his head. "He's got as many layers of anonymization wrapped around him as you had. As far as I can tell, he didn't have much in the way of detection running. He shouldn't have been able to tell much about your connection. In fact, he may not have been trying . . . if he assumes you're coming in from Breathing Space, he probably thinks he knows their system so well he doesn't have to bother."

"If," Megan said.

Mark shrugged. "We can't tell for sure, so there's no point in worrying about it."

Megan was looking at Leif. "Are you okay? You look a little rocky."

"No, I'm fine. I just—" Leif laughed. "You'll think this is funny. But I hate lying. I'm no good at it. At least, I always think I'm not, though the people around me don't seem to pick up on that."

"Was he impressed?"

"I think so. There's going to be another interview."

"Same 'street corner'?" Mark said from his workspace.

"As far as I could tell. He didn't give me any directions."

"Good," Mark said. "We'll need to record that one, too, since he didn't actually offer you any work or go into details about it . . . just said he might. But that'll be all we need to sink him, Megan."

"Not quite all," Megan said. She looked over at Leif. "It's not like I don't think you can handle what's coming up. I know you can. But now we're getting close to material that could get really hot . . . and I think if we don't go see James Winters first, before the second interview, he's going to be really, really cranky."

Leif nodded. "So let's call the man in the morning," he said, "and make an appointment. We're gonna catch us some big fish . . . and we'll let Winters bring some tackle of his own."

8

The view of James Winters's office, early the next morning, was probably not too much different from that of
anyone else in Net Force: plain institutional desk and
chairs and "filing cabinets," slightly dusty Venetian blinds
drawn against the sun coming in the windows this time
of day, the desk all scattered with solid datacarts and printouts and scribbled notes. But the ordinariness of it was
a surprise, since Winters was fairly highly placed in that
organization. Indeed, some people who didn't know better
would probably wonder why someone with such career
prospects, a decorated Marine as well as a very senior
member of the organization, would have taken on such a
relatively unimportant job as running the liaison office to
the Net Force Explorers. Just a bunch of kids, after all . . .
But Megan knew that this man did not hold the thousands
of "kids" he worked with as some kind of ornamental
junior auxiliary or publicity stunt. He was as serious about

his commitment to the online world and the business of making it safe and keeping it that way as he knew they were. It made dealing with him a touch easier . . . because he was a man of formidable personality, a little scary sometimes. Megan never went into his virtual "office" without twitching a little, for he expected his contacts among the Explorers to behave as professionally and proficiently as his senior agents. The idea seemed to be that, if the Explorers were careful and lucky, they would be senior agents some day . . . so getting a head start on the expected behavior was a good idea.

Megan's problem at the moment, as she and Leif waited in her workspace "on hold," looking at a dimmed-out view of Winters's office while he was briefly absent, was that she wasn't sure they had started the "professional" part of this particular escapade soon enough. Once or twice in the not too distant past, she had erred badly by refraining from calling Winters and Net Force in because she had seriously believed that she was handling everything just fine by herself. Now Megan was trying to be very virtuous about assessing her situations, aware that making the same mistake twice could be seen as fatal in this organization . . . and in dealing with some of the clever, unscrupulous and deadly lawbreakers that Net Force met during the course of its policing, often enough a repeated mistake *would* be fatal. *It really should be all right*, she told herself while she paced around on the worn marble of the amphitheater floor. *No one's done anything really dangerous . . . yet. I think.* The problem was that what someone in her late teens considered "not really dangerous" could sometimes clash spectacularly with the opinions on the subject of someone in his forties, who had seen too many of his people, over the last ten or fifteen years, fail to return from interventions—

"Nice view," said James Winters, having walked "out of the air" and into her space, wearing shirt and tie and dark trousers, with the unfakeable Net Force ID hanging from his pocket. His office now appeared undimmed and seemingly adjacent to Megan's space. "Sorry that took a little longer than I thought it would. It's been a busy morning."

Leif's space was also "adjacent" to Megan's at the moment, and he slid down off the hood of the Ice Cadillac and came into Megan's space to face Winters with her. "Morning, Leif," Winters said, peering past him into Leif's space, without comment for the moment. "Your dad in the country at the moment?"

"New York, sir. At least, he was there this morning at breakfast. . . ."

Winters made a wry expression. "The story of all of our lives. You never know where you're going to be when it's time for the next meal."

He looked over at Megan again. "Which of you wrote the precís I just read?"

"We both did," Megan said.

"Good," Winters said.

He turned and walked a few steps to reach back into his space, grabbed something in the air Megan couldn't see, and pulled it into Megan's workspace. It was a text window which must have been free-floating in the air there. Now it became visible to them, too, and Meg got a glimpse of the content scrolling past in the window and recognized what she and Leif had sent Winters earlier, a document describing as dryly as possible what they had been up to. "The first question I have for you," he said, "is—have there been any new developments in this situation since you filed this with me?"

"No, Mr. Winters," Megan said. "We didn't want to move any further until we heard from you."

"All right," he said. "That was a good idea." And Megan relaxed a little. "Let's look at possible options—"

Then one side of Megan's workspace, over toward the

right side of her desk, suddenly turned into the same swirling default blue that she had seen when Mark had touched base with them earlier. Mark walked out of it, and said, "Sorry I'm late. Dad was using the mobile."

Winters raised his eyebrows at Mark. "Was he calling the Sureté to come and take you away, do you think?"

"Huh?"

"Huh, he says." Winters threw Mark what Megan's father would have described as "an old-fashioned look." "Mark, you really want to check out the differences between the French laws governing online 'sovereignty' and the North American ones. While I understand what you were doing in Breathing Space last night, and I acknowledge that it may do some good in the future, in the present you have under French law committed an act corresponding to criminal trespass—"

"I wasn't entering any system of theirs!" Mark said.

"Yes, but you entered Breathing Space from an access point based on French soil, and you did it without legal authorization, without a search warrant from any online or other jurisdiction! That makes it not just entering, but *breaking* and entering with assumed/implied intent to defraud or steal. Cyberburglary. No matter that you did it in a good cause. If the French authorities find out, even your father's influence may be insufficient to keep you out of the pokey, because it's not the English/American modality of law they practice here, it's the Napoleonic one. You are presumed guilty until you can prove yourself innocent. Which you're *not*. And you've made these two accessories after the fact. Are you *listening*, Mark?"

He was. Mark was about as pale as Megan had ever seen him. She was sweating herself, but there was still something slightly amusing about it. *Or there will be if we're not in trouble . . . !*

"Yes, sir," Mark said, in a surprisingly small voice.

Megan blinked. She had never heard Mark call *anyone* "sir."

"So," Winters said, "let's see what kind of order we can bring out of this chaos . . . seeing that we have the data to begin with. And the implications are serious . . . but in their way encouraging, since it confirms suspicions that some of our operatives have expressed in the past."

"You've been working on Breathing Space already?" Leif said.

"Not specifically. But there have been too many reports of minors, or even juveniles, being caught up in international 'business' where they have no business being," Winters said, pushing his hands into his pockets and walking across to the edge of the amphitheater to look out across the bleak abruptly curving wilderness of crags and crevasses and methane snow. "Mostly it seems to have been courier work. The classic 'deadfall' routine; give a dangerous package to someone who doesn't have a clue what it is, so that if the authorities catch them with it, they take the fall, not you or the person for whom it was intended. Or worse, camouflage a parcel as something else entirely . . . the way they used to send 'sensitive' documents which were no such thing. Or maybe they were, but they weren't nearly as important as the microdot masquerading as one of the periods on the paper. Either way," Winters said, turning back to them, "over the past several years we've had about ten cases of minors 'taking the fall,' being caught with materials associated with some hostile intelligence operation or money-laundering scheme, or getting involved in some other shady scam. Some of them have been in pretty bad shape when we found them. Some of them have been dead. And unfortunately we have made very little headway with our investigations, because the people behind this seem to have been exquisitely sensitive to which kids are real ones, and which ones are Net Force operatives who just happen to look and act very young." Winters got a rueful look. "It seems that in some areas, there's just no substitute for having been born in the last twenty years."

"So you want us to—" Leif said.

Megan saw the flash of annoyance in Winters's eyes and immediately wished Leif had kept his mouth shut. "I do *not* want you to," Winters said. "The people we're dealing with, whatever their purposes may be, are professionals at what they do . . . which is staying hidden, and getting other people jailed, hurt, or killed on their behalf. Usually kids around your age . . . usually ones who are at least nearly as smart as you are." He glanced at Mark. "Almost all of present company excepted. I would very much prefer to let our own people continue handling this."

Then he sighed. "Except that this is the first concrete indication that we've found of the intentions and methods of the people who might actually be running the 'recruitment scheme,' and that they're actually being somewhat structured about it, enough so to keep coming back to the same places. And they've been canny about it, too . . . recruiting from a 'labor pool' who because of multiple run-ins with the law or a long history of 'going missing' are already either discredited as witnesses, or already given up for dead . . . or in a position to be. Nasty, very nasty . . . and I want it to stop. Not least because what Breathing Space does, when it's working correctly, helps a lot of people, and I would very much dislike to see the whole operation shut down in an atmosphere of scandal. Especially since Net Force should have been able to crack this by now, and hasn't. Results speak loudest, and the excuses would ring very hollow . . . especially to the parents of those kids who never came home."

Leif opened his mouth, then closed it again.

Megan simply looked at Winters. Winters looked back at her, and after a moment said, "I'd be willing to hear your recommendations."

She thought for a moment. "While they were in the report we filed with you," Megan said, "I understand that you might have concerns for Leif's safety . . . and almost might be concerned that he may have had second thoughts since we filed. However—" She glanced at Leif. He shook his head. "I think you should let him proceed," Megan said.

"Why?"

"Because substituting a Net Force operative for me, even one wearing an identical 'seeming' that you're pretty sure can't be seen through, has too many risks associated with it," Leif said. "What if the interviewer detects a change in 'tone' from the one I used with him? What if the substituted agent messes up some detail in the scripted history I've been working with, and with which I've had a fair amount of time to rehearse? And most to the point— what if you can't find anybody as good with as many languages as I am? Because you can't."

"You know," Winters said idly, "smugness is a big failing in our business, Leif." Leif flushed a shade of red that clashed with his hair. "Especially," Winters added, "when coupled with being right."

He paced a few steps across the worn white marble, his hands clasped behind his back, thinking. Leif gulped. "I'm sorry," he said. "I didn't mean to sound that way. But if you scare these people off the nest now, it'll be months, maybe years, before they try something similar, and you know they won't try it in the same place. Drive them even further underground than they are already, and they'll just go off and pull the same number in Moscow, or Buenos Aires, or Beijing . . . and it'll take Net Force just as long then to get a handle on it as it's taken now, and maybe longer, because they'll have gone to a lot of trouble to cover up their tracks in some way that'll make it difficult or impossible to catch them in the kind of thing they're doing at the moment. If you're serious about stopping

these people from ruining any more kids' lives, tempo-
rarily or permanently, I don't think you have much in the
way of choices. Let us help you get the evidence you need
to put *these* operatives away, anyhow."

Winters looked at him, then sighed and took a few more
paces. "It's the problem with the Hydra's heads, isn't it,"
he said. "Cut a few of them off and five more grow back
for every one you chopped. But at the same time . . . that's
no excuse not to cut off the ones you find biting people,
even if it does make other crooks elsewhere more cau-
tious."

He glanced over at Megan. "This, of course, doesn't
solve your problem, does it? Your friend is still missing."

"Yes," Megan said.

"Doubtless you're hoping that when we arrest the 'bad
guys,' that under interrogation they'll let slip, or in the
process of 'plea-bargaining' trade us, information about
what happened to Mr. Kamen."

"I would hope for that, yes," Megan said. And she
swallowed. "But I wouldn't hold my breath. And I
wouldn't let it stop me from going ahead with what we're
planning."

Winters stopped and looked at her thoughtfully.
"Would you care to elaborate on that?"

She didn't want to . . . but this particular line of reasoning had been chasing itself around in her head for many
hours now, and there was no escaping from it. "I don't
think it's likely that Burt is the only person they've 're-
cruited' in the past week, or the past month," Megan said.
"There have to be a fair number of others. If these kids
are seen as a safe and easy way to pass confidential information around, avoiding the Net or other methods
that're more carefully policed, then there'll be a lot of
them out there . . . and because there are potentially so
many of them available, they may be seen by these people
as disposable. Yeah, worrying about Burt got me into this.

I'm still worried about him. But the important thing is to *stop* this. It's not just Burt's safety that's at stake. Other kids are out there whose parents may really want to get them back safe. Their lives deserve to be saved as much as Burt's. And saving them may make the people who started running this particular scam think again about doing it at all any more . . . especially if it looks like Net Force may actually be using kids our age in 'live' operations. They'll never know for sure, in the future, when they're about to be 'stung.' Strikes me as a good thing, whatever my personal feelings about my friend might be."

Winters gave her a long look, then went back to his pacing. "And you?" he said, looking over at Leif. "Do you agree with Megan's assessment?"

"By and large, yes."

"Care to poke some holes in it?"

"To what purpose?" Leif said. "The meter's running, as we say in New York. Besides, you have your mind made up already."

Winters stopped for a moment, stared at Leif, and then grinned at him. "Does it show that much? . . . All right, look. You're suggesting that we enact full surveillance on Leif's next interview with the 'Recruiters.' You know that, if it goes as planned and we succeed in making arrests, you'll have to testify in court, and that despite the usual precautions being taken to protect your real identities, this could possibly lay you open to, shall we say, 'recriminations' from the Recruiters' people at some later date. Or immediately."

Leif and Megan both nodded.

"Obviously you two are going to have to clear your further involvement in this with your parents," Winters said. "Better find out what the situation is with them, and do it quickly. As you say, the meter is running."

Winters turned to Mark. "I know *you* understand this, insofar as you understand anything legal, because, having been properly empowered by Net Force, you've already participated in such undertakings. We can safely assume that the security arrangements which already cover your mother and father can be assumed to protect you as well. Maybe someday you'll even do something to earn them."

Now it was Mark's turn to turn a discordant red. "Other than constantly manifesting a wild talent with computers which could turn you into our century's version of Professor Moriarty, if you weren't so clearly obsessed with being seen to be operating on the Side of Good."

"Professor *who*?"

Megan grinned.

"Little Philistine," Winters said mildly. "What *do* they teach them at these schools?"

"And as for being on the side of good—"

"Stop before you say something more incriminating than anything you've said so far," Winters said. "Which, admittedly, would take some doing. Remember, the Sureté are only a virtmail away . . . and there's a standing one hundred thousand Euro reward for turning in a cyberburglar in France. Comes to quite a chunk in dollars, at the moment. Don't tempt me. My back porch needs fixing."

Mark stood there and said nothing, looking extremely glum.

"So as regards your part in all this," Winters said, "the initial surveillance you did was, as usual, highly effective. Megan attached a copy. I watched it all. Very incriminating. Very promising. And totally inadmissible as evidence due to the illegal way in which it was acquired . . . and also inadmissible without a search warrant, which we are now going to have to get busy acquiring so that the next set of evidence also is not contaminated. I'll handle that end of things." He glanced at Leif. "You're still waiting for your notification of the time and 'place' of the next interview, I take it."

" 'Around the same time today,' they said. Nothing more specific."

"It'll do," Winters said. "I'll instruct the system to fast-track any message from you to me immediately, whatever I'm doing, as this whole business is very time-sensitive. I want to hear about this next meeting thirty seconds after you do, from inside Breathing Space's virtual environment if necessary . . . there are ways to pass the information that won't compromise you. We'll work something out. Mark, have you planted the necessary backup files to substantiate Leif's claim?"

"Uh, not all of them."

"What??"

"I was working on it earlier, by my dad came in and threw me off the machine. He needed it for business," Mark said, rather plaintively. "And anyway, I was having trouble . . . that's why it took so long to get started in the first place. The Breathing Space client data files are better protected than the virtual space is—a lot better. I think somebody screwed up over there."

"I wouldn't throw rocks if I were you," Winters said. "Get back online and deal with it. I'll have the Paris bureau deliver you another set of Net server hardware pronto, so you won't be interrupted; and I'll speak to your dad. What's your room number?"

"I don't know if it has a number. It's the Presidential Suite."

Winters smiled slightly. "Ah, the privileges of rank. How often during this stay has your dad actually been *in* that suite, though? Poor guy. Mark, why are you still standing here? Go get on with it, and hurry up! There's no telling what records the Recruiters are pawing through at the moment, and you need to be there first!" He cocked an ear at the empty air, and added, "The Paris bureau chief says that in ten minutes there'll be someone coming down in the elevator with one of the new Force Nine portable setups." Mark's eyes widened. "Don't let your father steal it. *And don't break the chair!*"

Mark turned and vanished hurriedly, looking both harried and very relieved. Winters turned to Megan and Leif, who had been watching all this a little wide-eyed. "Don't mistake what you're seeing," Winters said. "I know I'm hard on him, but he's in a unique position, and his folks are busy . . . and they're friends of mine. Heaven forbid he should get messed up because somebody didn't spend enough of the right kind of time with him. But that's what this is all about, isn't it?"

They nodded.

"All right," he said. "Good job, you two. Go get hold of your parents, get things sorted out. Have them call me if there are any questions. I'll be right here . . . I have about twenty things to organize and we can't move until they're all in place. So your recommendations are accepted in full. . . . God help us. Now get going!"

They went.

Schiphol Airport outside Amsterdam had once been a relatively small place, built after the war, reclaimed from the sea like so much other polder, and named for the medieval and Viking ships that they had found there, on the old sea bed, when they walled in the area and pumped it dry. Now a replica of at least one of those ships stood in the middle of the new Arrivals Hall built ten years ago—lean, mean and rakish, sail down but her oars all out, and the dragon prow very pointedly facing the "wrong" way, toward the sea and the outside world. But there was some appropriateness in that, since the Duty-Free area, now more than half the size of the whole airport area, had been relieving foreigners of their money as assiduously as the Vikings ever had, for many years—and with this difference, that mostly the foreigners turned their money over, not just willingly, but gladly.

Burt wandered through the Duty Free area with his eyes wide. It was acres and acres of polished white marble and granite flooring, a space that made you swear you could see the curvature of the Earth, and the whole thing dotted and scattered with shops selling everything you could think of. That was what Schiphol's main Duty Free Sales area was about. Once it had been a little thing, barely a twinkle in the airport designers' eyes. But over the last half a century it had grown like a very lucrative fungus, spreading itself over many hectares of airport, so that the actual ticketing concourses and arrival and landing gates were now like mere tendrils and fringes around the body of a large beached beast swollen with much cash.

Burt had at first thought that it was a pretty raw deal to have to do what his instructions entailed—which was to go to Amsterdam, get off the plane, stay for a night in the airport hotel without leaving the area, and then the next morning, having made his drop and a reciprocal pickup, get right on the plane and go straight home again. *My first time out*, he'd thought, *and what do I get to see? Nothing! Not a damn thing*. This realization, as he looked sleepily out the window that morning—gazing for the first time the end of hours of ocean against a strange new coastline—had so soured Burt's mood that the approach to Dutch passport and control and customs, which would normally have made him appropriately first-time nervous, now merely made him want to snarl. In that he was exactly like about nine-tenths of the other passengers getting off the KLM red-eye flight out of Reagan International, and possibly for that reason Customs paid Burt almost no attention at all, past waving him through the "blue channel" with barely a glance or two.

Burt had gone gladly enough to the hotel and had had a hot shower, and then had fallen gratefully into bed, getting the sleep which he had not been able to get on the plane due to a mixture of excitement, nervousness, and a seemingly never-ending background of crying-baby sound effects. When he woke up, and realized that it was about five in the afternoon Dutch time, and he couldn't leave the hotel, then he really began to be annoyed. There was, however, nothing he could do about it. He wouldn't be paid for this work until he got home; he only had enough credit on the debit card they had given him to pay for meals and some drinks and his hotel room. He didn't even have enough credit to pay for a Net call home . . . not at the rates they charged here. The rates posted on the very basic little Net cubicle across from the shower room had made him blanch, even after he did the Euro-to-dollar conversion. Burt had been entertaining the idea of how much fun it would be to call Wilma from a public booth, from *Amsterdam*, both to let her know he was okay, and to completely astonish her. They had used to talk together about how much fun it would be to go overseas. Neither of them had ever envisaged being able to do it any time soon. *But here I am*! Burt thought.

For all the good it does me. I can't go see anything worth seeing. This is a waste of time. . . .

Still . . . there was the money to think of. He thought about it, and watched the local TV news in the cubicle, becoming increasingly fascinated by how strangely like English Dutch sounded sometimes. He looked at various other entertainment channels available, including one pay-per-view channel which caused him to turn so red with astonishment and embarrassment that he actually bolted the Net cubicle. Apparently the Dutch were amazingly liberal about some intrapersonal relationships . . . And finally, after going down to the hotel's twenty-four hour café and having a big plate of a smoky sausage called "rookworst" and a Coke, he had given up and gone back upstairs to sleep again. His plane back to Reagan was at lunchtime the next day. He would go to the airport early, he decided. It had to be more interesting than the hotel.

Now—standing in the midst of that vast, polished, glittering space that was the main "sales hall" in Schiphol Duty Free—Burt realized that he had been understating the case somewhat. There was more stuff here to buy than he had ever seen in one place in his life. Jewelry, clothes, liquor, watches, cameras, vidders, tricams, sound systems, porcelain, crystal, gold by the gram, ounce or kilo, diamonds by the carat or gram—He had stopped to stare in front of a little open-countered stall where a handsome young woman in a trim Schiphol staff uniform was weighing an emerald-cut diamond the size of Burt's thumbnail for a young man, while his girlfriend pored over another part of the case where still bigger ones lay under the security-wired glass, each in its little box, each labeled for size and brilliance. Burt had lingered there for a while, wishing he could bring something of the sort home for Wilma. But he didn't even have to look at these to know that their prices would turn him a whole lot paler than the ones on the Net cubicle back in the hotel.

He turned away regretfully, checked his watch. *The pickup's ten minutes away. Better go put myself where I'm supposed to be . . .* He started walking the eighth of a mile or so to the place where he had been told to wait, looking as he went at the stall next to the diamond place. There was a large rectangular hole in the floor, there, and Burt stopped to look at it curiously as a discreetly hooting klaxon began to sound. At the desk in front of the hole in the floor, a man in a dead black sliktite was bent over some paperwork, signing it, as the glittering new car he had just bought ascended from out of the depths to be examined before it was crated up and put on the man's flight out.

I want this, Burt thought. *I want to live like this. I like this kind of life!* Not that he had had much of it himself, so far. But he had seen other people living it now . . . and that was enough for him. He would do as much of this work as he had to to keep on living this way. No life Burt had ever thought possible for him at home had had this kind of wonder about it. It was uncomfortable, too, but it was worth it.

Burt made his way to the spot where he had been told to make his pickup—a fast-food shop owned by a famous chain. Burt hated their hamburgers, but he had been told to buy one, and which table to sit at to eat it, with his carry-on bag on the seat beside him. Then he was to go to the newsstand five stores down from the hamburger joint and buy a copy of a magazine called *Paris-Match*.

He did all these things, though he had never cared for hamburgers, finding them too greasy. Afterward, the rack carrying *Paris-Match* was well toward the back of the newsstand, and Burt had to go digging on the shelf for it, as someone had piled copies of some noisy yellow tabloid called *Blick* in front of it. He had put his bag down by his left foot, and was watching it out of the corner of his eye, so that when another bag that looked just like it appeared there, having been placed there by the owner of a very shapely pair of legs in blackline stockings, Burt was not surprised. After a little while the stockings moved away, their owner having picked up Burt's bag in exchange for her own, and vanished.

Shortly thereafter Burt squeezed his way back out to the front of the newsstand, between a number of other people who had appeared there, paid for the magazine with his debit card, and went on out into the concourse to see if his flight had been called. He knew from what he had been told that he should have had little time to do anything but go straight to his gate after making the pickup. But the big holographic display hanging in the middle of the sales hall, and automatically "repeated" in smaller versions down the length of the hall, said "delayed" in several languages. Burt sighed and went to the men's room.

Inside the stall, he sat down and stared at the bag. He had been told not to look . . . but he couldn't help it. What was the point of doing this kind of thing if you didn't have a hint of what was going on?

Very quietly Burt zipped open the bag. There was another jiffy bag in it, identical to the last one, but he had felt the difference in the weight of the bag the moment he picked it up. Burt peered into the bag, then took some toilet paper and used it to protect his hands as he pulled the jiffy bag out of the overnighter.

The jiffy bag wasn't closed. Burt peered into it. Inside was something which appeared to have been vacuum-sealed in heavy clear plastic. It was a brown substance. He couldn't smell anything, but Burt could see a faintly fibrous structure. . . .

Burt sat there and just went cold. He had always laughed at people's description of the blood draining out of their faces and down to his feet, but now he felt it happening to him, and he wasn't laughing. He was no expert on drugs . . . but this was what either marijuana or hashish looked like when you pressed it down tight and vacuum-packed it: Burt had seen enough news broadcasts featuring seizures of the stuff to have at least this much of a clue about what he was carrying.

Now he broke out in a genuine cold sweat. Burt had told Mr. Vaud that he would never ask questions. At the time he had meant it. But now everything had changed . . . for everyone knew how carefully flights that came in from Amsterdam were checked. There were old drug connections there that never went away, no matter how the Dutch authorities tried to stamp the trade out. An old tradition of tolerance for the "soft" side of the culture had created tremendous problems for them, adding to the ones already in place by virtue of the Netherlands' position as a country on the coast.

Why didn't this occur to me before? The answer was

simple. Too excited, too glad to get away to think things through . . .

And what do I do now?!

Burt glanced hastily around him for places he might "lose" the package . . . but then he let out a long breath, for there was no way *that* was going to work. The courier who would be expecting to make his pickup would be waiting for him on the far side of U.S. customs, Vaud had told him. If he didn't have the package . . . it would be very bad for him. Burt shivered.

Yet at the same time, he was sure that something just as awful would happen to him if he went through U.S. Customs, and if one of the people there, possibly just by looking to see how nervous Burt was, should ask him to stop and be checked. The sniffers they were using these days were delicate and accurate beyond belief: if one of them took a smell of his hands, there would be no question of what Burt had been in contact with, toilet paper or no toilet paper. He would go to jail for about a million years. And Wilma . . . what would Wilma think, when she heard about it on the news?

Why have they done this to me?! I was doing what I was told! I cooperated with everything!

Why?

And what do I do now?

9

Megan had often suspected her father of some level of affiliation with Net Force that had never been made fully plain to her, and probably wouldn't be for a long time . . . if ever. It had occurred to her privately that being a writer, with the freedom to go places without warning and investigate almost anything with no better reason than "I'm writing a book about it," would be a very useful cover for someone who was actually doing a whole lot more than writing a book about it. But she had never said this to her father, and she wasn't going to start now. She simply got out of the Net, went straight down into his office, and said, "Daddy, James Winters said I should talk to you."

He was sitting in the implant chair with his head leaned back, eyes closed, lips moving slightly—she had always teased him about being, not a lip reader, but a "lip writer." He liked to dictate, in his own virtual workspace, walking up and down and telling his stories out loud to an audience. Now the lip motions stopped, his eyes opened, and he looked at her with some mild concern. "About what?"

She told him. It took very little time. The thought of "the meter running" was very much on her mind.

As Megan talked, her father swung himself around on the seat of the implant chair, so that he was sitting more or less "sidesaddle," and looked at her in silence. "He said if there were any questions, you should call him," Megan said.

"Well," her father said. "I guess the *immediate* question is, why didn't you give me or your mother a hint that this was going on?"

"Daddy, I know," Megan said. "I'm sorry. It's just that all this started happening so fast . . . if there'd been a little more time I would have told you. But we had to start moving or we would have lost our chance to do anything useful. . . ."

Her dad sat there for a few moments and looked off in an unfocused way into the air. "You really are worried about Burt, aren't you," he said. "It's not just you trying to keep Wilma off your case."

Megan's eyes went a little wide at that. She had hardly spared a thought for Wilma since this business had started getting really busy. "Uh. No," she said. "Not that. It's just that Burt is . . . Burt's not used to this kind of thing, Dad! And stopping these people is the best way of finding out what they've done with him and getting him home again. Assuming he wants to come home. But he just ran away because he was unhappy, Dad. He doesn't deserve to get kidnapped or killed because he made an error in judgment!"

Her father didn't say anything for a moment. "Normally I would consult with your mother about something like this," he said at last, "but I get the distinct feeling from you that time is short. And to a certain extent, I agree with you . . . and there's probably not too much that can happen to you while James is riding herd on you both."

He chewed his lip for a moment. "Go on, then, get on with it," he said, mostly to Megan's back. She was already halfway down the hall to the other machine.

"Thanks, Dad!"

"I'll call school and tell them you won't be in," he called after her. "But tell Winters I'd appreciate a call from him when the excitement dies down. . . ."

"I will!"

Megan threw herself into the seat, lined up her implant, and went virtual.

Elsewhere in the virtual realm, Mark Gridley pressed himself up against a wall in the darkness and tried very hard to be still and small and nonexistent, for the monsters were after him.

Naturally they were not really monsters. The physical shapes presently stalking him were symbolic representations of the hunt/trace/immobilize routines that the programmers responsible for Breathing Space's client data storage had erected as protection around their clients' confidential personality-profile and counseling records. The routines had been written in a new release of Caldera II, the Net programming language that Mark knew and liked best. Unfortunately, they also incorporated some of the newer features of Caldera, ones with which Mark was presently not as familiar as he was with the older version of the language. As a result, the dragons had so far chased Mark three times right around the system firewall, knowing that someone was trying to get in and get at the files, but—because of the "cloak of invisibility" nondetection routine that Mark was wearing, they were unable to do anything more concrete about him than keep on following the "scent" his attempts to subvert the routines were leaving in the system. You couldn't rewrite code without leaving a trace, and the hunter/stalker guard routines were all too skilled at detecting that trace, that "scent," and following it. Every time they detected it, Mark had to move. If the routines actually came in contact with his virtual self, he would be thrown right out of the system, and he didn't have time for that right now. Time was, in fact, getting desperately short.

He kept on trotting around the firewall, which manifested, in an access of some programmer's rather skewed wit, as an actual wall of fire. *If there's a big rock in there with a Valkyrie sleeping on it, I'm leaving*, Mark thought. But leaving was very low on his list of things to do. He had to get in, and fast. The people he was expecting were certain to be along any time now.

He paused, looking at the fire, watching the pattern of it, the way the flames wavered. Behind him he could hear the dragons snuffling along, getting closer. But for a moment he ignored them. The flames did indeed have a repeating pattern. The anti-incursion routine meant to keep intruders out was cyclic, a single piece of code, recursing itself. The programmer was trying to save space, Mark thought. Not a terrible idea, usually. Could have been very elegant. But he stopped too soon. He should have hooked a random-number generator into it as well. He didn't, though, and the cycle is processing, canceling itself out in places—

The snuffling behind him, around the curve of the firewall, was getting louder. Mark ignored it, concentrated on the pattern. He had seen girls getting ready to jump into a double jump-rope in motion doing this same kind of pattern analysis with the body as well as the mind, looking for the open spot, the rhythm in which it repeated. Miss it and the ropes would clip you hard enough to raise a welt—or, in this case, the firewall routines would grab your Net persona, fling it into a "holding area" from which there would be no escape, and call the cops. *You dumb thing, I* am *the cops*, Mark thought. *Or I will be as soon as Winters gets the subpoena!* But even Winters couldn't get something like this handled instantly. Judges are not ordered around at will by law enforcement organizations. And this business was as time-sensitive as it came, unfortunately not even to be handled by a friendly call to Breathing Space. Too many layers of explanation to work your way up through, not enough time. Company was coming, would be along any minute now. And there was no more time. Mark swayed forward and back with the rhythm of the flames wavering in front of him. No more time, no more time, no more *time—*

He jumped through, came down wrong, sprawled. But it didn't matter. He was inside.

He ran across the landscape inside the wall of fire, a forest of trees which were actually tree structures. Great, a programmer who thinks that the pun is the highest form of humor. But it made Mark's work a little easier. He touched the hole of each tree he passed, and the labeling glowed through the bark, showing names and intake dates. The most recent ones were closest to the wall. Mark found the one that matched the time period that went with "Dawson's" back story, three months old, then poked the tree with one finger, and said to it, "Down."

Obligingly it sank into the ground like an elevator until Mark said, "Stop." He found the "D" branch and reached under the "cloak of invisibility" for what he had brought with him, the file confirming Leif's backstory. Right now this was still shaped like a manila file folder, but Mark looked at all the other files hanging off this branch of the tree structure, and grinned, for they were all in the shape of leaves. He twiddled the file in his hands, and it changed shape, shrank, went small and green and pointy, like all the other leaves. With care he held the file near the branch. A bare twig grew out to it, met the leaf, joined onto it. Mark took his hand away, and the leaf held.

And then he heard the voices . . .

Ohmigod, Mark thought.

"Up!" he whispered. The tree shot back up to its original level, almost dislodging Mark as he scrambled further up it like a panicked squirrel, hiding himself away up in the leafy branches, well above the dates involved in "Dawson" 's records. There he crouched on a high branch, as close to the trunk as he could get, and held very still.

Underneath him and not far away the fire died down, and two men in armor of the kind mistakenly called "chain mail" came stalking through it. They both had helmets on, hiding their features. These were symbols for "seeming" programs which were running concurrently with the "armor" routines that were protecting them from the fire. *Inside job*, thought Mark immediately. *Crap!* Someone inside Breathing Space had freely given them access to this data.

"Do you know where it is?" one of the men was saying.

"Are you kidding? Week in, week out I am in here . . . I know the place entirely too well. Right, here we are." The armored figure reached out and poked the trunk of the tree Mark was hiding in. "Down—"

Down it went, so that Mark's poor stomach complained bitterly, and he clutched the trunk and tried to keep absolutely still and silent. "Let's see now," said the man, feeling along the branches of the tree no more than six feet under him, while Mark urged him silently, *Don't look up, don't look up* . . .

"Aha," the man said, "here we are." He reached to the leaf which Mark had placed there only a few seconds before, and plucked it.

"Reading mode," he said.

A text window appeared in the air near him, and the man turned to it and began to read. "Yes, yes," he said as he read. ". . . Yes, all very unfortunate . . ." He made a couple of *tsk, tsk* noises as he read. Then he stood there, silent.

"So?" the other man said. "What's the problem? We have to get going, we have his interview shortly."

"I wonder if we should," the first man said.

"Why? What's the matter?"

"The date stamp on this file is wrong," said one of them.

A cold chill went right through Mark. "What?"

"Look at this," the man said. "The file was accessed only this afternoon. Only a couple of hours ago, in fact."

"So?"

"So why *would* it be? Why would anyone access this particular file at this particular moment in time?"

"Good question. Routine reevaluation?"

"Hmm . . ."

Mark swallowed, trying to do it quietly, and nonetheless convinced that the entire planet could hear him.

"Three months after intake date."

"See, there you are. Routine."

"I don't know. . . ."

"You're too suspicious. Come on."

"I stay free by being too suspicious. No . . . for me, this clinches it. Let him go, I don't want him."

"Isn't there a better way?"

"Such as?"

"Send him out, get some work out of him, and *then* lose him."

"Oh, like this last one."

"Yes."

A long pause. "It would teach them not to try planting anyone on us, wouldn't it." Then that man laughed softly. "All right. We'll 'hire' him . . . but his employment will be brief."

"Plants, though," said the other man. ". . . Now *there's* a nasty thought."

"Oh? What?"

"That last one, the blond boy. If this one is a plant . . .
that one could be, too."

The first man laughed out loud. "Him? You're kidding.
He barely knows what's happening to him. That's what
you said made him so perfect for the present job."

"Yes, I know. All the same . . ."

"Oh, come on, forget it! He's history now anyway, or
about to be so. Stop worrying and come on. We don't
want to keep our new 'employee' waiting."

"Where were you thinking of sending him?"

"That cash drop. Kiev."

"You really *don't* want to pay them, do you?"

"Increasingly, no. What better way to avoid it than to
have someone kill the courier, and then claim thieves did
it? And over there, it's the perfect excuse. They're all the
time stealing from each other, that lot. We get the money
back, though they don't know that; we set them at odds
against each other, which can only be good for us. And
we also avoid having to close a deal that was going sour
anyway. Gangsters, the whole lot of them. I hate giving
them good money that they don't even know how to launder properly anymore."

"Well, yes. Cash is tight all over. . . ."

They walked away, casually chatting about the murder
of other human beings, and Mark hid there up in the
branches of the tree structure and shook with rage, most
specifically because it had never occurred to him that *this*
was a place where it would have been a good idea for
him to have been "wired for sound." What he had just
heard would have been enough to put these men away
without Leif ever having had to take his meeting at all.
And now it was lost, evidence that could only be given
as his word against theirs. . . .

Mark let out a long breath, waiting to see the fire spring
up again, a sign that they were gone. Then, "Down," he
said to the tree, "slowly." It obeyed him, and he headed

for the firewall himself, intent, whatever happened, on not missing the meeting that would follow. . . .

You're going to come to no good end, was one of the lines that Burt always heard from his father. Well, now it looked likely enough that the old man was going to be right, and that left Burt absolutely infuriated. He had been right, and Burt had been wrong, for all Burt's natural life; and now Burt was going to be dead, and his father was *still* going to be right. It was too much to bear.

"You never could think worth a lick," he heard his father saying. "Never think things through. Just go charging in, don't get your story straight, don't have a clue what's happening until it starts happening. And then it's too late, because the ones who've done the thinking have already outthought you. Why didn't I get a dog and shoot the dog?"

Burt was going alternately hot and cold with rage at the familiar words, and at how for once they seemed justified. He sat there in the departure lounge which had been assigned to his KLM flight, and twitched. The passengers' baggage had already been X-rayed and metal detection done at the entry to the Duty-Free area. At least Burt was in no imminent danger of being caught with this stuff on him. But shortly they would get on the plane, and in seven hours they would be back in the States, and Burt would get off the plane and be caught with this stuff. . . .

You never could think worth a lick.

Burt sat there and burned hot with rage. *Why me? Why are they doing this? I was doing what I was told.*

Plainly they counted *on me to do as I was told.*

But why? *Why hire a courier and then throw him away after he's done what he was supposed to do?*

Burt stared out the plate-glass window revealing the broad expanse of Schiphol Airport, all that green grass under a blue sky, all incredibly flat. *Why—*

He could just see himself getting off at Reagan, going through customs. And then getting caught. There would be a big deal: *look at this, look what we found in this kid's luggage*. All the faces turned accusingly toward him, all the eyes staring—

And then, as he saw the eyes, as the sweat of humiliation and fear broke out on him again, Burt also saw something else. The eyes, the attention . . . and someone else slipping away in the middle of it all.

I'm not the important one on this plane! I'm just a distraction!

Someone else here has something much more important than I've got. They're going to get through when I don't.

Suddenly it was obvious. If Burt got caught, then whoever was on the plane and was carrying something much more important, much more valuable or more seriously contraband, would slip on by, be out, be gone, while Burt was still being strip-searched and flashrayed and probably just about turned inside out. Whoever this person was would have to be carrying the stuff in their cabin baggage, or on their person. They couldn't afford to have to wait to claim their luggage. It would be someone who only had carry-on.

Burt looked at his fellow passengers in near-despair. He didn't have any baggage to check, himself, and so hadn't had to stand in line at check-in and see who had checked their baggage in and who hadn't. And everyone here had some kind of carry-on with them. It was hopeless. . . .

Hopeless. And frustrating, knowing that right here with him, one of these people had something really illegal or dangerous, and they were going to use Burt to cover their escape, and get *him* caught instead.

An irrational impulse to start grabbing people and shaking them, one by one, and shouting, "Why are you doing this to me!" washed over him and almost immediately passed. That would be really stupid. Get him caught right now, probably. A bad idea. Yet at the same time, the urge to confront the person who was doing this to him, just by looking at him or her, would not go away.

Crazy idea.

Nonetheless, for lack of anything better to do, in the face of that DELAYED sign and the thought of his last few hours of freedom, Burt started to do it. He decided that he was not going to be obvious about it. But he was going to look every single passenger on this flight in the eye, and let them know that he *knew* what they were doing, what was going to happen to him. One of them would have to get the message. If the other two hundred or however many of them thought he was a little crazy, so be it. But he was going to have this last small satisfaction.

Burt started moving gently around the departure lounge with the overnight bag slung nonchalantly over his shoulder, positioning himself in one spot or another, and looking at people, systematically, starting near the door through which they would all board their plane, and working his way toward the door through which people entered from the main concourse. That was so he would be able to look at all the people inside, and when he'd looked into the eyes of every one of them, he could do the last ones in by standing at the entry door as they came in.

Burt made a game of it, working not to be obvious about it. Mostly people looked at him, bored, and let their eyes drift away. A few stared back, then lost interest. It went on that way for about fifteen minutes, as Burt moved as unobtrusively as he could from one spot to another, meeting the eyes of his fellow passengers, studying them all for signs that this person was the one who was going to betray him.

And then, maybe a hundred and fifty people along, he noticed something odd. There was a man in a long leather trench coat, a piece of clothing that Burt immediately envied, so that his glance at the man lasted longer than it might have otherwise. But as the man turned, he avoided Burt's eyes. And as Burt tried to make eye contact with him again, not being obvious about it, but just persisting, it slowly became obvious to Burt that this man would not meet his eyes under *any* circumstances. He would not even look in Burt's general direction.

It got to be more than a coincidence, as Burt casually drifted around the lounge, positioning himself here and there, and watched what happened. There was just no way to get the man to look at him at *all*. No matter where Burt might stand, the man in the brown leather trench coat, the man carrying the brown leather briefcase, the dark-haired man with a very ordinary face, simply was always looking somewhere else. Trying to get this guy to see him was like trying to look at the back of your own head without a mirror.

The uncertainty started to become certainty, and the certainty started to become triumph. *That's him*, Burt thought. *This is the one. No one else.* Somehow he just *knew* he was right.

The certainty made him almost giddy with relief. *All right*, he thought to himself, severely. It was almost his father's tone of voice, but newly made his own. *Let's think this through. Don't get all excited too soon. Fine. So this is the guy. What are you going to do about it?*

Burt withdrew behind a nearby pillar and looked at the man, while trying to seem as if he had his attention bent elsewhere. The guy had a briefcase, pretty much like anybody else's. Fine, but there could be all kinds of things inside a case like that. Burt thought of the diamond he had seen being weighed for that young guy back at the stall. That gem alone could have been worth tens of thousands of dollars. Five or six of those, tucked away in a briefcase full of important-looking papers, or hidden in some part of the briefcase less obvious—that could be very, very serious money.

But whatever he was carrying, he wanted nothing to do with Burt. That was all that mattered. Now all Burt had to do was figure out what to do with the information. . . .

"Figuring out" isn't your strongest suit, my boy, he heard that old familiar voice saying, amused, triumphant.

Burt frowned.

We'll see about that. . . .

10

Shortly thereafter, Megan flagged her system as "busy" to all callers and got ready to lie in wait. It had taken some doing. "This is my operation," she said. "It's my friend. I want to be in at the end!"

"There's nothing for you to do, Megan," Winters had said. "Leif is going to handle it."

"If I don't get to watch it go down," Megan said, "I'm going to—" Then she stopped, for she didn't know what she was "going to." And it was foolish to try to threaten this man. For one thing, she intended to be working with him some day, and for another, it made her sound juvenile.

Megan shut up and just looked at him.

Winters just looked back for a moment. "Oh, all right," he said at last. "There's a place you can sit and watch . . . with a few hundred other people."

"A few *hundred*??"

"This case calls for an unusual amount of oversight," Winters said. "As you'll see. Come on, I'll drop you where you need to be. Once you're put there, stay put! I'll be off making sure the surveillance is all in the right places, with the supervisory personnel from Breathing Space and the other jurisdictions all in place. And, by God, after all this they'd better be—"

Megan went with him, her heart racing.

Leif was sitting in the plaza in the same spot he had been in yesterday, drinking an orange juice and twitching. And without any particular fanfare, the man came walking across the sunny plaza, past the big bear sculpted out of blond wood that stood down at that end of the plaza, and stepped into the shade of the umbrella that sheltered Leif's table. Vaud just stood there for a moment, looking down at him thoughtfully. Then, "Prompt," he said "This is good to see. Will you follow me?"

He headed toward the restaurant, as he had done before. Leif got up, leaving his drink, and followed him. A moment later they were in the swirling "default blue" space again. Once again there was a chair set on one side of the table, but this time there were three chairs set on the other side. Vaud sat down in one. A moment later a couple of other men entered the space as Leif and Vaud had, and seated themselves.

"My associates," Vaud said. "Mr. Tessin, Mr. Grau."

They didn't give Leif the slightest sign of personal acknowledgement. They simply looked him over as if he was merchandise. One of them was a small man, round, balding a little on top, dressed in a more modern business suit than Vaud's; he had extremely blue eyes, and a face that had a fair number of smile lines in it, none of which were being used at the moment. The other man, tall and slender, seemed somehow to have his face in shadow even though the lighting in here was even enough. *Part of his seeming*, Leif thought. This gave him the shivers, for some reason. There was no reason the man couldn't have manifested a face that was normal, but just not his.... *That's the point, then. It's meant to give me the shivers. Very cute.*

"I would like to pick up where we left off yesterday," said Mr. Vaud, looking at the man whose face was in shadow. "There was some question about fluency."

"Whose, *mine*?" Leif said, genuinely outraged.

"Who else's?" said the slender man, Mr. Grau, in Moscow-accented Russian. "I am interested in your technical vocabulary."

Why, for courier work? Leif thought instantly.... *Unless this isn't about courier work at all, now.*

They suspect something. They think maybe I'm a plant. The idea assaulted him, all at once, and suddenly simply seemed true.

Great. Which way do I play this?

Leif's mind raced. There were two possibilities. Hide some of his own acuity, make it seem like he wasn't so strong on the tech side. Or let it shine—for technical vocabulary in all his "primary" languages was a matter of pride for Leif. *No way to tell which will work better ... not by myself, not right this minute. Let it shine.*

And so he did, for Grau began firing electronics and comms jargon at him, first in Russian and at high speed, then in German and even faster, sentences that were phrased as hard questions full of three-foot-long German "portmanteau words," big compound structures some of which were familiar to Leif and some of which were plainly being composed on the fly. Leif translated and answered as quickly as he could, consonant with using the words correctly—once or twice he had to use terms with which he wasn't familiar in a way that suggested he understood them even when he wasn't absolutely sure of the meanings.

And it went on that way for nearly another half-hour, grueling, veering without warning from language to language until Leif started to sweat. But shortly he realized that this test was not so much about his linguistic acuity, any more, but about his reaction to stress. Then he relaxed a little, and started to answer, purposely, more slowly, and with a little more arrogance. These guys were going to have to do better than this if they thought they were going to upset him.

Finally Grau stopped and looked at the others. "Well?" Tessin said.

"Adequate," Grau said.

And now I'm supposed to get mad. Yeah, right. Leif folded his arms, leaned back in his chair, and simply looked back at them casually.

Tessin nodded, looked at Vaud.

"Well," Vaud said. "The Russian in particular is good. And we have a delivery that needs to be made out that way. Gentlemen?"

The three of them looked at one another. Then Tessin and Grau nodded.

"Very well, Mr. Dawson," said Vaud. "We wish you to collect a package from someone who will meet you at Reagan International. Details of this will be virtmailed to you—but you must not use the Breathing Space account to access the information. Go find a public booth and access the address we are dropping into your Breathing Space virtmail now." Tessin nodded, the gesture of a man who has just seen to some matter. "You will be leaving tomorrow."

"So what's the pay?" Leif said.

Tessin smiled slightly. "The eagerness of the young," he said. "Well, this is your first time out, so it is lower than usual. We will see how you do. The price goes up somewhat with continued successful deliveries. Six thousand on departure . . . six thousand on return with the package that will come back."

Leif thought about that. "I'm not sure it's enough," he said.

The men all looked at him in open astonishment. "Goodness," said Vaud, "I would think you might feel that we were already doing you enough of a favor."

"So you might," Leif said. He thought for a moment, then said, "Fifteen thousand. Split half and half, as you say."

Vaud's expression went back and forth between annoyance and a kind of skewed admiration. "Oh, go on," Tessin said, "we can well afford it."

The other two paused, then nodded. "If you will pass us your account information," said Vaud, "we will have the system pass the funds to whatever cash card you use."

"It's a BlueChip card," said Leif, and rattled off a twenty-digit number. "I'll wait."

"My, what a young mercenary," said Vaud, genuinely annoyed now, but Tessin laughed. "Give me that again," he said.

Once more Leif recited the numbers. Tessin repeated them softly, under his breath, and then added something else that Leif didn't hear. "The transfer is being made now," he said.

Leif pulled out the virtual "twin" of his BlueChip and thumbed it on, touching in his PIN number and then glancing at the little screen which contained his balance. Even as he watched, it went from three digits to four before the decimal point.

He looked up, smiling happily. "Okay, Mr. Winters," he said.

The three men looked at each other. "Winters—" said Vaud. Tessin and Grau were already on their feet, fleeing out of the blue space and into the sunlit plaza. Leif lost sight of them as they went out. Vaud followed them fast. Leif went after.

Vaud was hurriedly threading his way among the tables, like a man constrained by Breathing Space's own virtual structure so as not to be able to simply vanish, but to have to leave via a prearranged "emergency exit." *He should have put it closer*, Leif thought with some amusement, as one of the people sitting at one of the tables he passed now stuck a foot out and simply tripped him.

Virtual experience may filter pain, and did so in this case, but not actual physical motion, which obeys the laws set up by the local programmer. Vaud scrambled to his feet and started to run again . . .

. . . and someone else jumped up from another nearby table and straightarmed Vaud right into the table opposite: he crashed into it, went down.

Vaud was good. Even as glasses and plates and cutlery went crashing to the pavement, he came up rolling, bounced to his feet again and started to dash off through the crowd in the plaza . . .

. . . only to discover that it was not a crowd as such, as yet another person bodyblocked him to a stop. Vaud stood there, panting, as the group of "diners" nearest surrounded him. Suddenly all their clothes showed an astonishing sameness—the primary "seeming" they had all adopted for this particular online intervention, under the "secondary" street clothes: the light blue, midnight blue, and silver of Net Force uniform. The whole expanse of Barenplatz was full of Net Force operatives, all now suddenly having reverted to their proper daywear after having been in disguise a little earlier, and all looking grimly cheerful.

Vaud stopped where he was. Over his shoulder, among other Net Force operatives, Leif caught sight of Megan . . . and saw what *she* was wearing. He grinned, and changed his own seeming to match.

James Winters sauntered into this group.

"Well, we've been looking for you for a while," he said. "Nice to see one of these operations pay off, though God knows it took long enough." He shook his head. "And wouldn't Dickens just have loved this? Take the innocent kids, use them, throw them away. Or turn them not-so-innocent any more, farming them out to the nastier intelligence organizations and criminal gangs. Pay them a pittance, keep the big bucks yourself. . . ." He shook his head. "Well, I don't think you're going to be harvesting the 'orphanages' of the world anymore. We have about twelve different law enforcement organizations looking at your people's work right now. I think this is a scam that's outlived its usefulness. Certainly for *you*. Take him and his friends away, boys and girls. . . ."

The Net Force operatives closed in around Vaud: a moment later they all vanished together.

James Winters turned to where Megan and Leif were standing, as the operatives dispersed. "We got a clean line on where they were 'physically' during this little visit," he said. "Three locations: Prague, Helsinki, and New York. Tessin there was right around the block from your dad's corporate headquarters," he said to Leif, "not too far from Wall Street. That wants to be looked into."

Then he grinned rather ferally. "Nice job, though," Winters said. "Nice work, both of you. Though you turned a few of my hairs gray when you upped the price, Leif."

"Why do a deal right away?" Leif said. "I had something they wanted. And besides, it would have made me look too eager."

"Yes, well," said Winters, bending a slightly more severe regard on Leif. "*You* should talk. . . . So all right, maybe it *was* allowable as protective coloration, seeing what everybody else was wearing. Just this once. Now take those off . . . until you're entitled to them."

Obediently enough, though with a touch of regret, Leif

vanished his Net Force uniform, going back to polo shirt and jeans, and saw Megan revert the seeming of her clothes to the more normal sweatshirt and day tights that she had been wearing.

"But what about my friend?" she said, losing her brief smile. "What about Burt?"

"We have a couple of guesses where he is at the moment," Winters said, and smiled again. "We'll confirm them if we can with Mr. Vaud. I think he's likely to prove talkative enough. So let's get on with business. . . ."

The process of getting off the plane seemed to take forever. It was amazing how long people could take just to get their bags together and walk off a plane without getting in each others' way.

Into the crowd of people standing around the baggage claim area, surrounding one of the carousels, came stumbling a tired looking young blond man carrying an overnight bag. His stance and gait suggested that he was desperately weary. He was, having been thinking with desperate speed for the last seven hours . . . but he wasn't tired enough so to make him stagger. Ahead of him, the man in the trench coat was stuck in a tangle of luggage carts behind some people who were trying to reorganize their bags on those carts, while waiting in line at the exit to drop off their customs declarations with the U.S. Customs people at the desks between them and the exit doors. Burt came slowly along behind the man in the leather trench coat, though not too slowly, and yawning.

Without looking at Burt, but as if he knew he was there, the man speeded up a little, as if trying to make it up to one of the Customs desks before Burt. The guys at the desks were looking at the people they were then dealing with. Not one of them, as far as he could tell, had even seen Burt yet, and they were not noticing what was happening behind the people right in front of them.

Burt stood there, wobbled, swayed . . . and fainted.

Or at least it looked that way. He simply pitched himself forward, not trying to catch himself with his arms at all, and plowed right into the man. Burt had played enough football in his life to make sure that his weight hit the guy right in that spot in the small of the back where it's almost impossible for the unfortunate person tackled to save themselves from falling. They either go down or hurt their back real badly in trying to prevent it. The guy started to go down, and now came the tough part, as Burt fell down on top of him, twisting rightward and sideways as he went, pushing the bag rightward, sideways, and most important, *under* . . . so that when they finally finished falling, the overnighter was mostly under the guy, and his briefcase had gone skidding right across the floor.

That got the attention of the Customs guys. The two of them who were processing people directly in front of Burt and his target looked up. The Customs agent immediately to their right, who had just finished dealing with somebody, now came around from behind his desk at the sound of the exclamations of the passengers behind them and the sight of Burt falling. He helped Burt up.

"Oh, he dropped his bag," Burt said. "I'm sorry, mister, look, there's your bag—" And he pointed to the overnighter, which was mostly under the man in the trench coat.

"That's not mine," the man was saying, shaken, "that's not my bag, where's my—"

And it was immediately obvious why he might have said something like that, for the overnighter's zipper had been open when Burt dropped it; and protruding from it now, sticking partway out of its jiffy bag, was an object which could not possibly have been mistaken for anything but a large rectangular lump of brown stuff with a texture like that of a good fudge brownie.

Now Burt stood there brushing himself off, and wondered in sheer terror whether this was going to get him in even more trouble. After he had decided to try his chances at changing the situation he was stuck in, and had decided on a plan, he had spent an uneasy few minutes in the one of the airplane's toilets with the overnighter—using one of the disposable, thin plastic toilet—seat shields to cover his hands while he wiggled the contents of the jiffy bag halfway out of it. He didn't know if he had contaminated himself again in the process. All he had thought at the time was that he was going to be in trouble no matter what happened, and it would be stupid not to try to alter the situation a *little* in his favor.

But now the Customs agents had the bag with the drugs in it, and were peering into it in greatly increased interest; and to Burt's utter astonishment, the man in the leather trench coat actually tried to push one of the agents away and run out through the door into the arrivals hall. The Customs agent grabbed him, and was joined a moment later by another one.

The passengers all around stared at this. And suddenly there now seemed to be about twenty Customs agents concentrated in a relatively small area. *Where did they all come from?* Burt wondered.

One of the Customs people, glancing around, said, "Okay, folks, come on, give us your cards and go on ahead. . . ." And several others of them led the man in the brown trench coat away into a small side room. One of them, holding the overnighter in rubber gloves, followed them.

Burt stared at this, too; then, as unobtrusively as he could, he attached himself to the confused family who were going past the desks now, the ones with all the baggage. They had several older sons, and some of these guys were passing in separate declaration cards for themselves. So Burt simply went in last after the third son, and passed his card in, too, as if the bags that went with it were on one of the carts. The agent who was taking the cards now just stamped Burt's and waved him on through, her attention rather more focused on the door through which her colleagues had taken the man in the brown trench coat.

Burt was shaking harder now, and hoping it didn't show, expecting every second that somebody was going to say "Wait a minute, kid. . . ." from behind him. But no one did. That was nice, but it was not the end of his troubles. For just past the Customs area door, probably, was the person to whom he was supposed to pass on his package . . . the package Burt didn't have any more. They would be waiting for him . . . and Burt was sure that when the man in the brown trench coat didn't come out, that other person would almost certainly figure out what had happened . . . and would not feel very kindly toward Burt. *I have to get away. But where . . . ? How? . . .*

He brushed blindly through the crowd of taxi drivers and car-service people who were standing outside the Customs area, holding signs, some paper and some electronic, on which appeared the names of passengers who had yet to come through. Burt didn't stop, and didn't look at any of them, for any of them could be his pickup, the person he now desperately didn't want to meet. No one followed him right away. But this was no consolation. It was still hopeless. He had no money left. There was nowhere for Burt to go.

Except the one place they didn't expect he would be likely to go, under any circumstances, considering that Burt was a runaway . . .

He hurried across the arrivals concourse to where there was a line of public-access Net booths. The first one he came to was engaged. Burt gulped and went on to the next one, and the next, and the next, and they were all engaged. There were footsteps coming fast behind him, but he didn't look back at the source of them, he didn't dare. *Never look back, they might be catching up.* The next one was occupied. And the next. *Oh, come on, what*

are all you people doing on the Net, don't you have lives!
Burt thought, and put his hand on the last one—

AVAILABLE, read the little green glowing sign over
the door.

He threw himself into it, shut himself in, and threw the
lock. There he stood trembling, half-waiting for someone
to start banging on the door.

"Megan," he breathed. She was a Net Force Explorer.
He had teased her about it enough times in the past. Now
maybe it would come to something. He felt around in his
pocket for his local-access comms chip—it seemed about
a hundred years since he'd stuffed it into his pocket on
leaving home—and threw it down on the booth's reader
plate.

Everything went white as the Booth's Net hardware
locked on to his implant and pulled him into synch. "Welcome to—"

"Abort start sequence, contact now, preset, Megan," he
said.

"Trying that connection for you now."

And there she was, standing in front of that big fat
planet Saturn. "Megan, listen, I'm in—"

—and with a horrible sinking of his heart he realized
that he wasn't looking at the live Megan, but her answering routine. "—can't come online right now, but
please leave a canned message or virtmail, I'll get back
to you—"

"Kill it," he said to the booth, and the image of Megan
whited out. "Dial—"

It was awful. He was almost ready to name his home
address—but not quite ready. *Not even for this*—

And then someone *did* bang on the door.

Burt gulped and did the one thing which he suspected
the person outside had no idea he was likely to do, under
the circumstances. "Nine one one!" he shouted.

The emergency locks on the booth's door engaged.

"State the nature of your emergency!" said a dry female voice out of the whiteness.

"There's someone trying to kill me," said Burt, "and he's going to get away with it unless I talk to someone from Net Force right away!"

"Where are you, sir?"

"You know damn well where I am," Burt said to the unseen voice, "you've got this booth's Net address right in front of you right this minute, and if you don't let me talk to someone from Net Force in the next thirty seconds, I'm going to be dead shortly, and probably a lot of other people will, too, pretty soon, so *get on it!*"

"Connecting you," said the voice, rather hastily.

Burt smiled rather grimly as the world blacked out around him and the hardware in the booth made the connection with his implant. *Dad's voice again*, he thought. Yet there were unquestionably some things that it was good for. Now he could only hope that those things would happen fast enough. . . .

Megan blinked her implant off, sat there in the chair, and just let out a long breath. There was nothing more she could do, not for the moment. She had to just relax and let matters take their course. *Relax*! she thought, amused at herself, for she was trembling all over with reaction. "Yeah, right."

She got up and stretched. "Boy, could I use some tea," she said, and headed down the hall; past the bathroom, where at least one of her brothers was having one of his legendary hour-long showers; past the den, where her dad was in the chair, talking to somebody; into the kitchen, where various Day-Glo water sports gear was draped over the kitchen chairs. Apparently Mike was thinking about going kayaking later today.

The doorbell rang.

"Oh, great," Megan said, and went to answer the front door.

There was a man standing there, wearing a business suit—a shortish man, dark-haired, with one of those faces you would pass on the street and which would leave no impression. "Megan O'Malley?" the man said.

Oh, no! said some part of Megan's mind, very loudly.

And she hit him. Right there, with full straight-armed extension, with the heel of the hand; right in the good spot, the spot where her martial arts instructor had strongly suggested she not hit anybody unless she really meant it, since the move actually veered a lot closer to unarmed combat than any martial arts move, and unarmed combat (unlike martial arts) is about having people not get up again after you hit them.

She heard the man's sternum crack. He fell backward down the stairs.

Oh, no, she thought, going no more than one step after him, and there falling into ready position, just in case he should try to get up again. But he showed no signs of doing any such thing. *Oh, please don't let me have ruptured his pericardium*, Megan thought, for that was always a danger when you played around with the sternum. Your opponent could bleed to death in a matter of a minute or so. *Or bruised his liver—*

"Megan," her father said, very calmly, from behind her. "One step to the left please, dear."

She turned. Her father was holding what was usually kept locked in its safe in the den, a firearm of truly monstrous proportions, to her mind anyway, and it was leveled at the man's head. Megan gratefully took one step to the left.

"Megan," said Mike, coming around the corner of the house from the garage side at a dogtrot, holding a kayak oar with what looked like very unfriendly intent, "you've *gotta* stop doing this stuff to the magazine salesmen. It's not their fault."

"Megan," Sean said, appearing behind her father with a towel wrapped around his middle and completely dripping wet, "how're we supposed to beat up the people who beat you up if you won't *let* them beat you up first? We never get a chance to do the brother thing anymore."

Megan stood there, breathing hard, and smiled.

"Your mother's going to be furious that she missed this," Megan's father said mildly. "As for you, sir, I suggest that you lie very still and try to keep the writhing to a minimum, as I or one of these extremely dangerous and uncontrolled youngsters might be forced to construe some sudden motion of yours as an aggressive action, and then to do something we'll all regret later. Though as a family we would certainly be sure to send flowers afterward. Megan, is this one of your threesome?"

"I don't think so. Net Force accounted for all of them," Megan said. "But he's nobody I *do* recognize, and why should anybody I *don't* know come here looking for me right this minute? But look, we'd better get him to the hospital—"

"Panic button's hit," Sean said, pushing his wet hair out of his eyes. "Let him lie there, the professionals'll handle it. Our legal liability is now limited. Dad, did he make an aggressive move just then?"

"Wishful thinking, son. Go put some clothes on. Response time is down to about a minute these days, the ambulance'll be here soon enough. Ah—"

But it was not the ambulance. A big multipurpose vehicle with the Net Force stripe and logo came howling down the street and pulled up in front of the house, and even before it stopped, people with various kinds of armament even bigger than her dad's were piling out of it. They surrounded the man lying at the bottom of the steps, and shortly another Net Force van arrived, with an ambulance in tow. A stretcher was produced, and the man was transferred to it and thoughtfully restrained. The handcuffs were probably just an afterthought.

And within about five minutes the vans were all gone, leaving behind them just a quiet suburban street with about fifteen different neighbors standing out in their front lawns or on their front sidewalks, staring at Megan and her father and her brothers. "We're going to hear about this from the neighborhood association again," her father said wearily, turning to lock the handgun away again. "They'll accuse us of lowering the property values around here."

"Idiots," Mike said, heading around the house again with his kayak oar over his shoulder. "Megan's just making the world safe for democracy again."

"Yeah," said Sean, and took his dripping self back inside.

Megan stood there a moment more. "Dad?" she called after him, as she followed him into the house. "I take it back about the boys. They can live."

"Oh, good," her father said. "Funeral expenses are getting so unreasonable lately. . . ."

Late that afternoon, in Megan's space, she and Leif met with James Winters. The news had come through a couple of hours ago that Burt had been picked up at Reagan International by a Net Force flying squad. The D.C. police had the man who had been hammering on the booth's door. They were holding him on attempted assault charges for the moment, confident that they would shortly have something much better to book him on.

"Well, first of all, the Gridleys have now left France for Germany," James Winters said, sitting and admiring the view of Saturn in a chair which Megan had summoned out of the air for him, "so I suppose we can all stop worrying about Mark being sent to Devil's Island after all. Though he may wish he'd availed himself of that opportunity after his mother gets through with him." Winters's smile was dry.

"He won't be in too much trouble, will he?" Leif said.

Winters sighed and shook his head. "He'll be all right. He's plainly being saved for bigger things." He turned his attention to Megan. "Which brings us to you, for whom it seems the same could be said. But it all links back, as you thought, to your friend Burt. The operative chasing him had a 'listener' of a kind we haven't seen before. Net booths are supposed to be shielded against such things, but there's always somebody out there coming up with something new. . . ." He sighed. "He pulled Megan's Net address from the booth as Burt was dialing it. After that it was, as usual, all too simple for him to get your street address. . . . What went on in the guy's head after that, I'm not sure. He may have thought he could snatch you and use you to put pressure on us to release his associate, the man with the briefcase. Not that it turned out all that well for him." He gave Megan a rather cockeyed look. "You reacted fast. Maybe a little too fast."

"You try being born last behind four large and hungry brothers," Megan said, "and see how fast it makes *you*."

Winters produced a dry smile. "Point taken. Anyway, your reasoning about why someone unknown should show up there right then was correct enough. And I wouldn't worry about having him turn up on your doorstep any time soon—not that, after a welcome like that, anyone lacking a deathwish would be terribly eager to. Besides a very sore chest and a body-bruise you could paper a wall with, the guy's already got several counts of assault, interstate flight, various other black marks . . . We and the other law enforcement agencies will be having a series of long talks with him, and one or more of those will land him in some none too comfortable Federal retreat for a good while. Your guy in the trench coat may not spend that long on our shores, but that's only because of all the extradition arguments that are going on at the moment."

"Why?" Leif said. "What was he carrying?"

"If either of you spent as much time watching the news as you do working on your hobbies," Winters said, leaning back in his chair, "you might make an educated guess."

They both looked blankly at him. "You really *do* need to pay more attention to the news," Winters said. "Two weeks ago someone shanghaied a bankers' courier outside the main train station in Milan. Dragged him off somewhere, then stuffed him into the trunk of a car that they left up near Udine somewhere, and went off with what the courier had been carrying—which was one point five billion Swiss francs' worth of 'white paper' negotiable securities. The police in Milan assumed that the thieves would run up into Liechtenstein with the paper—they're in a currency union with Switzerland—or maybe over to Jersey via France, and launder the paper by running it through one of the smaller merchant banks there, then moving the funds right along after clearance into various other jurisdictions, the Caymans, say, or Andorra. . . . But whoever was running this particular white-collar thief decided to try the 'hide in plain sight' maneuver instead. They told him to go to the U.S. via Amsterdam, and then arranged with your friend Mr. Vaud to put a 'disposable' courier on the same flight as a distraction." Winters shook his head. "Strikes me as an error in judgment. They should have covered him up a whole lot deeper . . . or alternately, they should have given your young friend Burt the paper. Who would have suspected him?"

Winters stretched and yawned. "But they outsmarted themselves. Always nice when they do that. . . ." He smiled slightly. "And you two are sitting pretty at the moment. If you want to go to Italy, I suspect the Milanese police would be willing to pay your airfare. That stuff was snatched on their watch."

Megan smiled. "Well," she said, "I'll see what my dad thinks." She sighed. "All I want now is to see Burt. I've had about six calls from my friend Wilma in the last two hours. . . ."

"I'll get out of here," Winters said, standing up. "Come on, Leif. Let's let real life, whatever *that* looks like, reassert itself." He looked at Megan with something she had never seen on his face before, something which brought her out in a hot embarrassed flush: just simple pride.

It lasted about a second. "I want a complete report from the two of you, with discussion of the sociopolitical ramifications, in eighteen hours," James Winters said. "See me in my office for critique and further discussion two hours after you submit it."

And he vanished.

Megan let out a long breath. *"Homework,"* she said with genuine loathing.

"Yeah, but *what* homework," Leif said. "I'll call you later."

And he vanished, too.

About two hours later Megan and Wilma and Burt were in Megan's space, sitting around and just reveling in things being a lot more normal than they had been for the past few days.

"I hate to tell you this," Burt said, "but even after all that . . . I don't know if I want to go home just yet."

"Nobody's going to make you," Megan said.

"But I miss you. . . ." Wilma said, She squeezed Burt's hand. The two of them had been holding hands almost constantly since Burt arrived, having been questioned by the police and released as soon as they had conferred with Net Force.

"I miss you, too. . . . But I can't go back there."

"Megan?" said what sounded like the voice of the Great and Powerful Oz.

"Yeah, Dad?"

"Can I come in?"

"Sure, come on ahead."

A moment later he was in her space and glanced over at Burt. "Perfect," her father said. "I hoped you were here. Look, Burt . . . You've been through a lot, and you've managed it surprisingly well. If you don't mind, I'd be happy enough to offer you a spare room for a couple of months. We're redoing the garage at the moment, since we haven't been using it. It's better than being in a shelter, no matter how humane the shelter is."

Burt shook his head. "Mr. O'Malley," he said slowly, "it's really nice of you . . . but I think the distance was doing me some good. I want to keep working with the Breathing Space people for a couple of months and see where it gets me. But I'll stay in the area." He looked over at Wilma. "We've got those qualifiers to think about in a few months, after all."

Wilma took his hand and didn't say anything.

"Everybody will be able to find me," Burt said. "I'll be getting in touch with my folks, all right. I have some things I have to say to them. Maybe not the things they think . . . especially my dad. But after that . . . We'll see. I can manage to finish school, anyway, if I don't have to go home at night. After that . . ." He looked at Wilma. "I don't know for sure. But we've got a while to work on it."

"Okay," Megan's father said. "That sounds good to me."

And he vanished.

The three of them sat there looking at one another. "So . . ." Megan said.

"So," Burt said. "Let me see how you've messed up

the sim of Buddy. Maybe if someone puts a real rider on top of him, we can get it fixed."

A moment later he was being assaulted by two young women. A moment later they dragged him off into another area of virtuality. Beyond the white marble amphitheater, the Sun dipped below the surface of Rhea, and very gently, all around, the atmosphere began to sublimate out in a low-G storm of bluish swansdown snow. . . .

PENGUIN PUTNAM INC.
Online

Your Internet gateway to a virtual environment with
hundreds of entertaining and enlightening books
from Penguin Putnam Inc.

*While you're there, get the latest buzz on
the best authors and books around—*

Tom Clancy, Patricia Cornwell, W.E.B. Griffin,
Nora Roberts, William Gibson, Robin Cook,
Brian Jacques, Catherine Coulter, Stephen King,
Ken Follett, Terry McMillan, and many more!

**Penguin Putnam Online is located at
http://www.penguinputnam.com**

PENGUIN PUTNAM NEWS

Every month you'll get an inside look at our upcoming books and new features on our site. This is an
ongoing effort to provide you with the most
up-to-date information about
our books and authors.

**Subscribe to Penguin Putnam News at
http://www.penguinputnam.com/newsletters**

In the future, computers rule the world. The Net Force was formed to protect us from any and all criminal activity on-line. But there is a group of teenage whiz kids who sometimes know more about computers than their adult superiors. They are the Net Force Explorers. They go where no one else can go. And they fight crime like no one else in the world...

Tom Clancy's
Net Force®
Runaways

After her equestrian teammate Burt disappears, Net Force Explorer Megan O'Malley finds him at a combined online-offline refuge for runaways. But Burt's next disappearance may be his last. Short of cash, he takes a job at a mysterious courier business—a service, Megan discovers all too late, to which many runaways are sent out, but few ever return....

$4.99 U.S.
$6.99 CAN